CARTER'S
BIG BREAK

CARTER'S
BIG BREAK

A NOVEL BY BRENT CRAWFORD

HYPERION · NEW YORK

TO SARAH AND THE BOYS

SUMMER

1. S'UP?

On the last day of school, I'm happily strolling down the hall after Mr. Rumpford's ridiculously hard algebra final. He told me last week that if I failed it, I'd have to go to summer school . . . as if! I studied so hard last night, I thought my brain would fall out. But it didn't, and I aced that sucker with a D+! I waited around after the bell rang and watched as Rumpford graded the tests. Yes, I had better things to do, but my summer was hanging in the balance, so I kind of didn't. I knew I'd passed when he looked up. He gave me a nod and said, "Imagine if you'd applied yourself like this all year, Mr. Carter."

I laughed at his joke, returned the nod, and replied, "Yeah!" as I headed for the door.

My freshman year of high school was "difficult," to say the least. I overcame a slight stuttering/confidence problem; I took on a couple of bullies; drove (perhaps wrecked) a car (and truck); figured out how to talk to/make out with chicks; discovered that hard work can get you through anything; and wound up with the lead in the spring musical (*Guys and Dolls*) *and* a hot-ass girlfriend. But Abby's not just a pretty face, great boobs, and a perfect butt. She's also ridiculously smart, reads books for fun, listens to cool music that they don't play on the radio, and watches movies that my boys and I would never see. They aren't even movies—they're "films," and most of them are so far over my head, I've got a neck ache when they're over. But after Abby explains the plot, I start to understand and actually enjoy the story long after the credits have rolled. I don't tell my boys this (especially EJ, my closest friend since birth), but Abby's kind of my best friend now. And she lets me touch her boobs, which tips the scales in her favor every time. My friends try to hate, and call me whipped because she holds my hand every once in a while, and I may have stood them up on a "bros before hos" night to play Scattergories with her. But whatever. I've accused enough dudes of being "on the leash" to know that my boys are just jealous.

In the weight room the other day, my friend Nutt's older brother, Bart, gave me some advice: "You gotta go off on that bitch every once in a while. . . . Just, out of nowhere, call her a whore. It keeps her on her toes and therefore . . . on your jock!"

Bart can bench 275, but I've noticed he doesn't have a girlfriend, and to my knowledge, never has. He claims it's his choice, but I've had one for about a month and it's been pretty sweet, so I'm going to hold off on Bart's relationship tips until I'm proven wrong.

I give out a few nods, high fives, and a bunch of "S'ups" as I make my way toward Abby's locker. I'm about twenty feet away when I hear footsteps coming up behind me, a little too fast for comfort. I squint my eyes and flex down because I know that someone is about to tackle, punch, or slap me. A sharp sting in the kidney region confirms my theory. I arch backward, scream in pain, and turn to find EJ, Bag, and Doc cackling with laughter.

"OOOOWWWWE!!" I exclaim, swinging my back-pack at all three of them.

EJ is able to ask, "You ready——?" before the bag nails him in the ribs. "HRUUAHHHH!"

I rub my back and reply, "Hell yeah. Are we rollin' out to Grey Goose Lake in the CRX?"

Bag replies, "Naw, we gotta ride our bikes. Hormone's dad is still pissed off about that cop bitching him out for givin' a fifteen-year-old a car."

"Still?"

Three weeks ago, Doc figured out that if you remove the windshield-wiper fluid hose on an '87 Honda CRX and angle it to the right, it will shoot pedestrians, cyclists, and unsuspecting drivers with surprising accuracy and force. You're pretty screwed if you want to wash your windshield, but if you want a laugh, pull up next to somebody and ask them to roll down their window.

Bag would say, "Pardon me, sir? Do you have any Grey Poop-on?" then, *SQUUUIIIIIRRRTT*, right in the face!

We shot everybody . . . including an undercover cop. It was super funny when the drenched officer was pushing Hormone's terrified face into the hatchback glass and yell-ing something about "vehicular terrorism" and asking us the obvious question: "What's so funny?!" Comedy can't be explained to her victims, and it's not nearly as humorous now that Hormone's dad has confiscated our wheels and we have to ride our bikes again. But it was hilarious at the time.

My boys join up for the last few steps to Abby's locker. My back is still stinging, but oddly, the pain in my ass is directly in front of me. Bitchy Nicky, Abby's best frenemy, is holding court, standing with my girlfriend and a few other random chicks. You never know from one day to the next if they'll be at each other's throats or BFFs. Abby and Nicky usually have a third member in their trio, Amber Lee. I was actually in love with Amber until she publicly screwed me over at the homecoming dance last fall. But she's been absent for the last couple of days, and because she was heard vomiting in the girl's bathroom last week, rumors are flying around that she's knocked up. You never know what to believe, because I've also heard that the baby is mine, and unless I missed something in that sex-ed video they showed in health class . . . that's as untrue as it is impossible. The movie was about fifty years old, but it still managed to give me a boner, which tends to distract my absorption of information . . . but I did not get Amber Lee pregnant.

Abby doesn't see me at first because Nicky is ranting about something or someone that's pissed her off. If you can't be happy on the last day of school, when can you? Her left hand is on her hip, and her right one is waving all around like she's a ghetto mama from the mean streets of Merrian, and not a cheerleader who's getting a car for her birthday and going to Florida for a vacation.

She points at Abby's nose and yells, "I'm all, like, 'Oh no, you didn't disrespect ME!'"

Abby is politely listening to the story that probably never happened. She's wearing a summer dress with a tank top underneath. It's not tight, but she pokes out of it in just the right spots. She's smokin' hot, and did I mention she's my girlfriend?! I fight off a smile as I walk up behind Nicky, put my hand on my hip, and start to act out her moves. I purse my lips and circle my head around, then check my fingernails and mouth her words as she cackles, "I kicked that fool to the CURB!"

Abby laughs like Nicky is the funniest comedian in the world before brushing past her and jumping into my arms. "Hello, lover!" she says as I spin her around like a pimp (not a guy who's trying not to fall down).

EJ rolls his eyes with judgment, but I don't care, because she smells so good and I'm proud to have a hottie in my arms calling me "lover," even if the term isn't exactly correct. EJ knows that she and I have not had sex yet, but he doesn't say anything, because we both know that, at the moment, I'm a lot closer to having *it* with her than he is with any other chick. So she can call me anything she wants!

"S'up?" I ask her.

"I've got the grade-school drama camp in a few minutes, and Ms. McDougle wants to see both of us. Can you walk me down to the drama department?"

"Sure," I reply as if I hadn't completely forgotten about her summer job teaching kids how to talk louder and sing all the time.

Abby kisses me again and squeals, "Did you know that the drama camp staff is made up entirely of college kids? They're all drama majors, and then me!"

If I was working off of Bart's advice, this would be a good time to call her a bitch or make fun of people who go to college and actually major in "drama." But I like seeing her happy, and kissing her, so I just say, "That's awesome."

Nicky finally butts herself back into the conversation. "ABBY! I was telling a story—"

But she's interrupted by a screeching boy sprinting

down the hall toward us. Jeremy is a drama geek but super cool . . . and super gay. He violently hugs us and gasps for air to deliver his news. "Oh my God, did you hear?!" he pants. "A movie—is being shot—at this ratty-ass school—in this Podunk town—this summer! I just heard—Principal Banks say—"

That's about all we can understand, because he starts hyperventilating like he's giving birth, while Nicky is trying, in vain, to finish her tale. But "Excuse me" is all she gets out before EJ swings his backpack at me.

"Dude, let's go!" he exclaims. His bag is filled with the entire contents of his locker, so he loses control of it when I step out of the way. He grips the shoulder strap with both hands and his body flails from the momentum. He sees the path of destruction before anyone else and closes his eyes with dread as the load smashes into Bitchy Nicky's chest and slams her into the lockers with a teeth-chattering *BANG!*

I instinctively point at EJ and go, "OOHHHH!!!" with everyone else. Nicky has no idea what hit her, but there is no doubt she soon will, and it's not going to be good for EJ. He's super fast, so he's able to grab the angry cheerleader before she crashes to the linoleum. His arms are wrapped around his overstuffed Jansport and Nicky's waist in a bizarre romance-novel pose.

He futilely cries, "Oh my God, I'm so sorry!!!"

Nicky is just trying to breathe and figure out what's happening to her. The weight of the backpack and the girl are too much for my boy to hold, but letting go doesn't seem to cross his mind, so they slowly slide down the face of the lockers and crumple to the floor. EJ and Nicky are nose to nose like unfortunate Siamese twins joined at the Jansport. The once-deafening hall is dead silent as we wait for her to claw his wide eyes out. He nervously chatters, "That was a total accident . . . It's all Carter's fault. . . ."

Nicky and I ask in unison, "WHAT?!"

"I cleaned my locker and my baseball cleats have mud in them, so it's heavier—"

She's still dazed, but notices all of the people looking at her, so she yells, "Get the hell off of me, FOOL!!!"

He finally releases her and stammers another apology before springing to his feet and awkwardly trying to help her up. He squats down and grabs at her armpits, but grazes boob on the way in. His eyes light up and he exclaims, "SORRY!" before wrapping his arms around her back to avoid a slap. His face knocks into hers as he hauls the confused, beaten, and mortified girl back to standing.

I offer up a fist bump and mutter, "Smoooth."

He leaves me hanging and asks her, "Are you sure you're okay?" as he brushes the hair out of her eyes.

She takes a deep breath, and with a red face, replies, "Yes, I'm fine . . . thank you."

My eyebrows fly up, and I look over at Abby for confirmation. She mouths the words "thank you" in disbelief.

EJ says, "It's not a problem. . . . You are very light and easy to lift and also very firm . . . to touch. So, I thank you."

She smiles, and the crowd groans with disappointment. I snap my fingers in his face. "Dude . . . I gotta go see what Ms. McDougle wants."

He's still staring at Nicky when he asks, "Huh?"

Abby jumps in. "EJ, why don't you get some ice for Nicky's head and a Diet Coke, maybe?"

EJ puts his arm around Nicky's waist and walks her toward the nurse's office. I shoot Abby a suspicious look. She giddily replies, "What? I think they would make a cute couple, and she could use a nice guy."

"What, to sacrifice?"

2. DOWN GETS OUT

Abby and I walk into the drama department holding hands. She's telling me about the French final she just "bombed," but I know she probably missed three questions and might have to suffer the humiliation of an A-.

I space off for a second and think about my dad's grand plan for ruining my summer. I was going to be a junior lifeguard at the pool, but I guess you have to be fifteen to wade around the baby pool and tell kids when to use the slide. Since I don't turn until the end of July, they rejected my application. My dad thought I was upset about not having a job, so he decided to take some time off of work and tear out our old deck to build a new one . . . with me. But I didn't want just any job; I wanted to be a lifeguard! I wanted to twirl a whistle, jump off the diving boards, and check out bikinis all day. He offered to pay me ten bucks an hour, which is twice as much as a junior lifeguard, but the work is going to be twenty times harder.

Abby says something in French and laughs at herself, but I don't speak French, and all I can think about is how to get out of this stupid deck venture. I tried to explain that I couldn't possibly help him because there's nothing wrong with the old deck, and deforestation is a very big problem for our planet. He didn't seem to buy it and told me that the old wood was totally rotten and that we were going to use recycled products on the new one. He was so proud of his arguments, but I shut him down. "I'm just too busy, Dad! I've still got to go to the pool every afternoon. And my boys and I are planning to work out at the Merrian High gym every morning so that we look swollen when we take off our shirts."

But he wouldn't listen to reason and kept yammering on about how much he's looking forward to hanging out with me, and how Lynn and I will be going off to college in a few years, and how fast we've grown up, and something slipping by us. . . .

Abby interrupts my thoughts by asking, "Can you believe that?"

"Nope," I instinctively reply as we walk into the classroom.

Ms. McDougle is standing in front of her desk, smiling from ear to ear. She bum-rushes us as we walk in the door. It's okay to hug this teacher because we're in the drama department and that's how they roll down here. She's crazy cool and obviously as fired up for this summer as we are.

She asks, "Do you guys remember that writer friend of mine who came to school in December?"

"C. B. Down?" I reply like a guy who knows writers, but I only know this one. His book, *Down Gets Out*, is my all-time favorite. Yes, it's the only one I've ever read, but Abby's read a million of them, and she thought it was awesome, too.

Ms. McDougle continues, "Yes, well, he's also a film director—"

Abby interrupts, "Yeah, his first movie just won the Cannes Film Festival!"

I ask, "It did?"

Abby adds, "Carter and I are seeing it this weekend."

"We are?"

She gives me a look and says, "Yeah, I sent you that article; did you not read it?"

"Oh yeah, that!" I exclaim as if I just finished it.

McDougle continues her story. "Well, the film rights to his novel sold, and he's going to direct the movie . . . right here in Merrian, this summer!"

Abby and I are giggling like idiots as McDougle fills us in on the movie details. "C. B. saw our production of *Guys and Dolls* and was so blown away by both of your performances that he wants you to audition for the lead parts!"

Everything after that sounded like she'd jumped in a pool and was talking to us from underwater. I love movies more than I can possibly explain. I believe she's describing the audition process and what a "producer" is, but I'm way too busy writing my acceptance speech for next year's Academy Awards. I'll have to ask Abby for the information later. I'll be sure to thank her in my speech.

McDougle hands us each a thick stack of paper that's bound with a black clip. I assume it's the screenplay, and I'd like to ask if I really need to read it, because I've already read the book, but I'm smiling so wide that my lips won't work. She tells us a few more things and then asks, "You got it?"

"Sure," I reply with Abby (whom I hope actually does).

I hug them both good-bye, because we're still in the

drama department, and grade school kids are starting to trickle in and things are about to get LOUD! I'm supposed to ride out to Grey Goose Lake with my boys, but I need to go freak out for a while.

I duck into the auditorium and bound onto the stage screaming, "HuuuuWHAAAA!!!" There's something about a theater that just gives you permission to lose your mind. I yell, "YEEESSSSS!!!" and "OH MY GOD!!!" to no one.

Playing Sky Masterson in *Guys and Dolls* was probably the most fun thing I've ever done, but I never dreamed that acting in the spring musical would change my life the way it has. And not just because my "raw talent" has been discovered by a film director. Doing that play ripped me out of my comfort zone and showed me that although my friends are awesome, I don't need their approval if I want to do something. Plus, they're going to make fun of me no matter what I do, so I might as well enjoy it.

I'm standing in about the same spot where C. B. Down read to us from his book. I totally remember the haunted look in his eyes that sent a chill down my spine and shut five hundred kids up instantly. It didn't hurt that he was a total bad-ass, like a UFC fighter blended with a rock star. He had full-sleeve tattoos and more ink on his neck and hands. His dreadlocks were pulled back into a ponytail, and a thick beard covered his chiseled face. His voice was soft and sounded like he'd been smoking a pack a day since birth.

I totally remember him reading to us from the first chapter. "The first time my parents left me alone, I was fifteen years old."

At the time, I chuckled, but then realized I'd never been left alone either. My older sister, Lynn, is always there to bitch at me when my parents are unavailable. Then he got into the point of his story, how he (Chris in the book) hadn't really been "left alone." His parents drove off of a bridge on their way home from a party. He's not sure if they did it on purpose, until the end of the book. Chris has to go live in a foster home, but he's a spoiled little bitch at this point in the story and can't handle it. He gets into a fight with his foster father and is told that he has to go live in a group home. His guidance counselor had warned him that he'd have to go to this tough-ass boys' home if he couldn't get along with the foster family and that he was too big of a pussy to live there. So, Chris takes off and comes to Merrian and squats in the basement of the scary old Saur mansion. This chick Maggie (Ms. McDougle, we assume) helps him out all the time, and he enrolls at Merrian High, gets a job at the Hy-Vee, makes friends, falls in love, starts writing for fun, and eventually wins a writing contest but gets busted as a result. I can't remember all of the details, but it's really good (way better than I just made it sound). It's funny because the kid on the cover of the book kind of looks like me, and when I was reading it, I always saw myself as Chris.

Abby told me that it's very common to cast yourself as the lead character in the book you're reading, and because she's a smart-ass, she added, "If you'd read more, you'd know that." *I wonder how common it is to actually get to audition for the film version of your favorite book, smarty-pants?* Abby also used to say that the story was "very Dickens." So that's how I would describe it to people who didn't know that I had no idea what or who "Dickens" was. Abby got me three of Charles Dickens's novels as punishment. I started to read all of them, but they weren't as good as *Down Gets Out*, so I didn't finish. I did find out that "what the dickens?" and "you little dickens" have nothing to do with that writer.

I'm rudely sprung from my daydream when my boys rush into the auditorium. Bag says, "I told you he'd be in here . . . drama fag!"

I snottily tell them about the benefits of being a "drama fag." "Have any of you jackasses been asked to star in a movie today?"

They may not love theater the way I do, but we all dig movies, so proper jealously flows my way.

3. HOW MANY FINGERS?

On the ride out to Grey Goose, I'm spacing off, polishing up that acceptance speech when EJ crashes into my rear wheel, and I almost wreck. He keeps riding like nothing happened, so I ask, "S'up, dude?!"

He looks at me, still lost in thought, and asks, "Yo, does Bitchy Nicky have a boyfriend?"

In unison, everybody yells, "NO, and there's a reason!"

We approach the ditch-jump behind Pizza Barn, and my friend Bag's about to turn into it so he can bust a cool trick like he always does, but I accelerate ahead and cut him off.

"What the hell, Carter?" he asks, as I angle into the yard and zip down into the ditch before anyone can say anything else or I chicken out. I'm known for being a bit of a wuss. Typically, I would go last off of a jump and only get a few inches of air, but I'm feeling like a million bucks today . . . and perhaps a bit overconfident. I pump the pedals hard as I make the approach. I hit the lip going ten times faster than usual, rock my weight back, and rip the handlebars toward my chest.

EJ and Hormone cheer, "YEEEAAAAHHHH!" as I launch into the air. So high. Way higher than Bag has ever soared. Way, way, WAY too damn high! This is the spot where a guy in the X Games would bust a tail whip, or go for the backflip, but I decide not to. I've got other things to worry about. Flying through the air is probably more enjoyable when you have some idea how you're going to land, but I don't. I simply start screaming, "HUUUAAAAAAHHHHHHHH!!!"

Intellectually, I know I should kick the bike away and try to land on my feet, but the signals are not getting below my neck, so I simply death grip the handlebars and watch the blacktop get closer and closer to my fragile, helmetless skull, and listen to the front tire violently *POP* and the metal frame *CRUNCH* beneath my weight. Then all sounds are drowned out by the *WHAAAAM* of my head hitting the pavement, and the chorus of ringing bells.

I'm fairly certain that I slid on my face for a few feet . . . but not a hundred percent. The rest of the bike wreck is pure conjecture, because my lights went out when the first bells started to chime, and I don't remember a damn thing.

A foghorn blasting inside of my head rudely wakes me a moment later. My body is twitching as my central nervous system tries to reboot itself. My eyes are fluttering inside their lids and I can barely hear Doc yelling, "Call 911!!!"

I'm trying to tell them that I'm fine, but I'm just moaning "Muggggeddiiii" instead.

"He's awake!" EJ gasps, and starts slapping me.

I try to block his shots and figure out what possible good could come from beating me as I roll around the dirty street. The ringing does get quieter as his slaps get stronger. He cries, "Stay with us, Carter!"

Finally my mouth works, and I yell, "Quit it!"

"He's fine," Nutt says, holding up his hand and demanding, "How many fingers am I holdin' up, Carter?"

I'm slightly annoyed because he's moving them all around, so I snap, "Four, dumbass!"

They all look at each other with concern before EJ adds, "That doesn't mean anything. Carter's always sucked at math."

After a half hour of playing, "How many fingers?!" and getting most of the answers right, we start walking our bikes toward Hormone's house.

Bag still wants me to go to the hospital, but nobody else wants to sit in a smelly waiting room on the last day of school, and Hormone thinks he can use me to get his car back.

They show his dad my mangled bike and face as exhibits A and B in the case of why we shouldn't have to ride our bikes anymore. He looks at me suspiciously because I'm leaning on EJ, and my left eye is blinking like I'm flirting with him. He asks, "Are you sure we shouldn't take him to the ER?"

"No, no, he's fine," Hormone assures him. "Show 'em, Carter . . . how many fingers?!"

"Three!" I declare.

I must have gotten it right because Doc adds, "See?"

Hormone's dad accepts the diagnosis as if the surgeon general had made it. He hands over the keys and tells us, "Stay out of trouble." Either that or he said, "Learn how to juggle."

We abandon our bikes, and Nutt calls "Shotgun" as we pile into the little car.

We're barreling down the street when I ask EJ, "Hmmm?" as if he asked me a question.

He looks over at me with concern. "Are you sure you're okay?"

For the hundredth time I say, "Yes."

Nutt turns around suspiciously and asks, "How many fingers?!"

"Shut up," I reply. "Where are we going?"

Hormone yells back, "Grey Goose Lake!"

"Why?"

Nutt answers, "There's a party."

"How come?"

EJ snidely replies, "We just wanted to do something nice for you."

I flip them off before taking a quick nap.

Twice more I wake and ask where we're going. EJ reminds them how forgetful I am even when I haven't hit my head. We pull off of the main road and park beside the Grey Goose Golf Course so that we can sneak into the lake area undetected by the security guard.

The next thing I know, it's dark outside and the CRX's dome light flickers on. My face isn't working right, and I've got a terrible HEADACHE. I hear EJ whispering to someone, "No, baby, it's cool. Carter's passed out . . . he won't mind." My left eye won't open, but my right one cracks just wide enough to observe Bitchy Nicky climbing on top of EJ in the passenger seat. I'm trying to shake away the cobwebs and figure out why I would be imagining such a horrific thing, as he shuts the door and starts sucking her face.

"Duuude!" I protest.

Nicky yells, "Get the hell out of here, Carter!"

I try to tell EJ he's making a big mistake, but nothing comes out when I open my mouth, so I just pop the hatchback and stumble across the golf course toward my party.

I'm headed for the lake to go for a swim, but my sister spots me fighting to peel off my T-shirt. I hear her laughing at my painful struggle. "Carter, are you drunk?!"

The neckline of the shirt scrapes my mangled face and causes me to gasp. Her eyes fly open as she barks, "Oh my God! Who did this to you?"

I point to myself, because I am, as usual, my own worst enemy.

I think that she dragged me through the party and showed her friends how jacked up I was. I bet she hunted down my boys and yelled at them for bringing me out here in this condition, but I'm not sure. I know that her boy-friend, Nick, gave me a ride home, because he carried me into my house and I was drooling/bleeding on his shoulder when my mom's screaming woke me up. He's, like, six-five, two-hundred-and-fifty pounds. He's going to play college football next year and he's really cool, so when my eye snapped open and I found myself in his massive arms like a little papoose, I had no idea how to handle the situation, so I just pretended to go back to sleep.

4. THE KIDZ CHANNEL

I took it easy on my first few days of vacation. I think it's called a "semi-coma" in medical circles, but my dad didn't make me work on the deck, and I had a chance to read the *Down Gets Out* script. I'm disappointed to find that it's really different from the book, so I call Abby to make sure I'm reading it correctly.

She's pissed off at me for not calling her for three days, but after listening to me mumble the excuse, she feels bad for me. She's also not happy about the script changes, but I guess Ms. McDougle explained all of the reasons on the last day of school. The story is less about the homeless kid and more about the girl who helps him.

Abby says, "It's because stories about empowered young women are very hot this year."

I mutter, "But that's not what the book is about."

"Well, you can tell C. B. Down and the producers at the audition."

"Maybe I will," I joke.

Sometimes she thinks I'm a complete dumbass, so she begs, "Please don't!"

She asks if she can bring me anything for my pain, so I inquire if there is any way she could get a hold of a slutty nurse's uniform and hook me up with a nice sponge bath.

She isn't really on board with dirty talk yet, so she just starts yapping about how busy she is with drama camp and drill team practice. We make plans to see a movie tomorrow so that she can see for herself how jacked up I am and give me some proper sympathy. She fills me in on more gossip about the movie: "The Kidz Channel is producing it," she says with dread.

"Cool! We might get to be on Kidz?"

"Not cool," she replies. "They have their own talent pool, but that's not what's got Ms. McDougle freaked out. She thinks they're going to cheese up C. B.'s story even more. It's supposed to be a Sundance type of film, not a Kidz movie, and just because it stars young people, they think—"

I cut her off, "What do you mean, 'their own talent pool'? Like, we won't get to audition?"

"No, McDougle says that C. B. really wants the producers to see what we can do, but because of all the money they are throwing at him . . . they're trying to force him to cast those Kidz Channel actors who've grown up in front of the camera. McDougle says they'll ruin the film with their bad acting."

"It's his story, right? He can do whatever he wants with it. That guy didn't seem like a sellout to me."

"It's the first film he's done with a decent budget. She says he's always been really poor, so he might not be able to handle it very well."

I start to freak out, but Abby tells me that there's nothing we can do except be great at the audition. We talk through the scene a few times, and she explains all of the weird script terminology. One of the drama camp guys has done some film work, and he was nice enough to teach it to her. The dialogue we're reading from is almost at the end of the movie. It's really short, and it seems to be an argument between her character, Maggie, and my character, Chris. The lines are really sad, too, because we're coming to the realization that we shouldn't be together anymore. The script says that I'm supposed to cry, but it doesn't say how I'm supposed to make that happen. Abby says I shouldn't even try, but it says it right there on the page: "Chris sobs." She also explains that her character is forcing my character to break up with her so that Chris can move on and accept the scholarship and not feel tied down. We go through all of the lines a few times and Abby sounds really good already. I, on the other hand, need to work on it. She tells me not to worry about getting too emotional or anything and to just keep it simple and see what happens. The lazy side of me wants to agree with her and just wing it, but there's this new side of me that's learned about the power of hard work and how effective it can be. My head is really starting to pound from all of the thinking I'm doing . . . that and the blunt trauma I suffered a few days ago.

She says, "Take some Advil, Carter. I can't wait to see you tomorrow."

I don't say anything for a couple seconds because I'm trying to read what's written on my hand. She reminds me with a slight tinge of bitchiness, "We're seeing a movie tomorrow, at one o'clock. Write it on your arm, please."

"Dude, I got it!"

The next day I wake to the sound of a saw ripping through the old deck and my mom yelling at my dad, "Knock that racket off!" I can tell by the tone of her voice that she's not angry with him for building a new deck, she just wants to make it clear that she's not helping with it. I go back to sleep for a minute but am awoken again by the sound of the car starting. Dang it! Mom and Lynn are going shopping and leaving me to fend for myself. I remove my crusty bandages for emphasis and go down to break the news to Dad that I can't help him today.

"I-I-I'm still in a lot of pain," I dramatically explain. "And Abby really wants to go to the movies."

He seems disappointed but doesn't make me help. He revs the saw and says, "You're going to miss the best part—demolition!"

I point to my swollen face and tell him that I'm sorry, before going inside to eat cereal and look at the audition sides again. I can't stop thinking about it. The dialogue is way better than *Guys and Dolls*, but it's that same kind of rapid-fire talking, so I know that I need to have the lines down pat. Ms. McDougle has trained us to analyze dialogue in terms of the emotions as well as the words. She always asks us, "What do you want from this scene?" But I have no idea what my character wants yet. I can tell that it's going to require a very subtle, passive-aggressive anger and various levels of hurt. I'm not sure how I'm going to play all of that, but I'll keep working on it until I do.

EJ skids to a stop in front of my garage as I'm inflating the new front tire my dad brought home yesterday. "You ready?" EJ asks.

"For what?"

He notices my pus-filled scabs and yells, "Daang, your face is gross!" then does a reenactment of the wipeout, complete with sound effects, slow-motion action, and instant replay.

"Very nice. What am I supposed to be ready for?"

He replies, "The movie!"

"No, dude, I'm seeing a film with Abby."

"So am I."

I shake my head. "It isn't a tricycle date; you're not invited."

"Yeah, I am. We're meeting up with her and Nicky at one o'clock."

"Bitchy Nicky?" I ask.

"Yep," he clarifies. "And don't call her that anymore."

"What do I call her?"

"Just Nicky, dude."

"That's not her name."

"Yes, it is. Actually, it's Nichole." He giggles.

I do a mean impression of his giggling, so he's aware of it and won't do it again. When his dumb smile has faded, I hop on my bike, and we roll out. I'm not trying to be a hater here, but EJ is making a big mistake, and I don't want to double-date with it!

As we ride he tells me, "Yo, you need a hat or an eye patch so Nicky doesn't freak out about your evil eye."

My mouth is still sore, so I just shoot him a dirty look, as if to ask, "Why would I do anything for that hose beast?"

EJ catches my meaning and replies, "She's got a nice ass!"

I cannot dispute that, but she's still the spawn of hell, so I mutter, "She was so mean to me last year—"

"Yeah, I think that's what makes her such a badger in the sack!"

Pain flies through my skull as my jaw drops. "Son of a bitch, you've already had sex?!"

"Hell yeah!" he yells, and goes to high-five me. "Three times!" he adds. I stick out my hand for the slap, because he's my boy, but I'd rather run him off the friggin' road. This SOB hooked up with Sara "the Caboose" Ruiz a few months ago, and then he got lucky with a drunk Hooker High slut at his church. The Caboose heard about the Hooker and cut him off, and I was secretly very happy about that because I was more than a little jealous. I had been slightly ahead of him in this department until he tapped the Caboose. But now he's pulling ahead of me like a race car from a go-cart.

"Did you or did you not *speak* to her for the first time . . . four days ago?" I ask.

"That is a fact." He beams.

"Man, she's a slut!"

"No doubt, but you can't call her that, either."

I shoot him another look.

"Dude, I need you to be cool to her," he says nicely. I'm considering his request when he looks over at me, puppy-eyed, and adds, "We're in love, man."

UGHHHHH, what the hell is wrong with this summer?

We pull up to the movie theater just in time to see Abby and Nicky hugging like long-lost friends under the marquee.

"Must be a friend day," EJ observes.

Abby looks super cute, so I pop a wheelie into standing and give her a painful kiss. "S'up?"

Abby notices my busted-up mug and gasps. *Finally. Thank you.*

Nicky's arms are folded when she snidely says, "You're late!"

I look at my watch and see that she is absolutely right . . . We're one minute late. I glance up from my watch and sigh, "You gotta be kid—"

Abby shuts me up by touching my bruised face and asking, "How's your face, baby?"

I flash a wincing smile because I was just referred to as "baby" for the first time since I was an actual "baby."

"It's killing us!" Nicky laughs like a horse and punches EJ in the chest.

EJ laughs his ass off at the lame joke his whore made, so I seethe, "Wow, that joke was funny . . . in sixth grade."

I cannot believe those two have had sex!

"Be nice," Abby says, grabbing my hand.

Nicky looks at EJ's bike, then at her manicure, and snickers. "I don't know why I thought when you said that you were 'riding bikes,' that you meant motorcycles. Of course you boys only have Big Wheels."

I ball up my fists to end this double-date disaster, when Abby jumps in to defend us. "Bicycles are way cooler than motorcycles. You get exercise and peace and quiet, and you're not destroying the environment."

"And it's not illegal for us to ride them," I add.

Abby finally asks, "What movie do you guys want to see?"

"*Cheer! The Musical!*" Nicky barks.

"Yeah right," I snort.

Nicky screeches, "EJ?!" in protest.

As if my best friend would side with *her* over *me* and see friggin' *Cheer! The Musical!*

28

EJ looks at Nicky's boobs and then explains to my Nikes, "Carter, um, Hilary Idaho plays the head cheerleader. She was always your favorite *Get Up Gang* member. . . ."

My left eye pops open for the first time in two days. "I do not, nor have I ever had, a favorite *Get Up Gang* member!"

The Get Up Gang was this morning show on the Kidz Channel that Lynn used to like, so therefore I watched. It was about this band of kids who lived in a cool clubhouse/loft and sang corny edited versions of gangster rap songs and worked out elaborate dance routines to them. I remember kind of digging a Halloween number, "99 Problems but a Witch Ain't One," but Lynn stopped watching when the gang took a field trip to Iowa, and they put on overalls and cowboy hats and proceeded to assassinate the old 2 Live Crew song "Me So Horny" by turning it into "Me So Corny." That was too much. The show was really popular, though, and those guys were everywhere for a while: magazines, cereal boxes . . . *America's Most Wanted*. This one kid, Tito, who wore an eye patch, died of a drug overdose, and they just replaced him with another one-eyed guy named Tito, like we wouldn't notice. They all seem so cheesy and happy on the show, but in real life they're always getting arrested or going to rehab. Every episode has a moral about "abstinence" or "truth and justice in the hood," but it's tough to sell honesty and chastity when mug shots and sex tapes keep coming out.

EJ is still pushing Nicky's agenda when he totally sells me out. "Carter had a poster of Hilary Idaho in his room!"

"My sister!" I bark. "That was Lynn's poster, and she had it in the bathroom to work on her makeup techniques!"

I did love that poster, though, because Hilary Idaho was

super cute wearing a private-school-girl outfit and leaning back on the teacher's desk. Her belly button was exposed, and I would get lost in it for hours. But that was years ago, and she was not my favorite *Get Up Gang* member. I actually liked Zac-Michael Wienus (lead singer and youngest of the Wienus Bros), because he was the smart-ass on the show and he didn't do all that silly mugging for the camera that all the Kidz Channel kids do. . . . But I'm not going to get into that with these people. He's Hilary's boyfriend, and his mug shot was just on the cover of *US Weekly*. He had this cool smirk on his face, like, "Whatever."

"I'm not seeing some refried cheesefest about singing cheerleaders."

Then Abby pipes up. "I guess *Cheer! The Musical* wouldn't be so bad. I'll probably have to teach some of the songs at drama camp, so . . ."

I shake my head and exhale my contempt when Abby kisses my bruised cheek and whispers, "We'll double feature C. B. Down's movie, *Genoa Eyes*, okay?"

I give her a wink, because I've been working on my winks, and ask the ticket girl for two student tickets and where they keep their crackers.

"What crackers?" she asks.

"The crackers I'm gonna need to stomach this cheesy movie."

EJ busts up, but then looks at Nicky to see if it was funny or not. Turns out it wasn't, so he stops laughing and shakes his head at me in disappointment.

Abby grabs my hand and asks, "Can I buy you some popcorn to cut the cheese?"

A fart joke! How cool is she? (I may have farted during

a movie last year, and it might have been so nasty that it caused her to barf.) I can't even fake being pissed off at her. I squeeze her hand and say, "There won't be any cheese cutting at this movie, and we'll need the popcorn as a prop for the double feature."

As soon as the lights go down, EJ and Nicky start making out. I'd make a move on Abby, but my face couldn't handle it. She probably does want to watch this crap for the songs and stuff, so I shouldn't just reach over and grab some boob . . . like EJ is doing before the opening credits! At a G-rated movie, he's over there making porno grunting noises. I nudge him and tell him to "Shhh!" but it doesn't do any good.

The movie starts out just as you'd expect. Cheerleaders are singing and dancing. Everyone's happy to be alive and smiling all over the place. Zac-Michael Wienus is the lead guy, and he's supposed to be the stud football player. (A hundred-pound gay-wad with a floppy hairdo and lip gloss.) On the Merrian High football team he'd get his ass handed to him if he shimmied under the center's butt and started gyrating his hips around and rapping about "scoring." I recognize all of the dudes from Kidz Channel shows. They're doing cartwheels over each other, and no one is smashing into each other properly. They're throwing guys into the air, and the opposing team is catching them to the beat. It's completely unrealistic and totally ridiculous and . . . I absolutely love it! I wish *I* could be on their football team instead of mine. Practice would be so much more fun. I'd be the best singing, flipping, linebacker/kicker of all time! Abby catches me bobbing my head to this song "Go! Fight! Win!" so I make a face and mouth, "Sooo lame." She laughs because she knows I'm a goof and she digs me anyway.

I guess I haven't watched enough Kidz Channel lately because Hilary Idaho has blossomed in the bra! EJ's busy right now, but we'll discuss this development privately, at great length, very soon. She's so hot! Tig ol' bitties, long hair and tan skin, and the girl can dance her ass off. She sings really great except for when she belts out a word like "Win" and adds fifteen extra syllables, so it becomes, "Weeeeiiiiiaaaahhhheeeeeiiiiiaaahhhhhuuuuunnnna!!!" The movie finishes up in exactly ninety minutes (so they can stick it on TV in six months) with the football stud, Zac-Michael, joining the cheerleading squad and helping them prevail in the national cheer championships. He hooks up with Hilary (just kissing, of course), and then they wrap it all up with a jazzier version of "Go! Fight! Win!" The picture freezes on the cheerleading squad in mid-gayness, standing on each other's shoulders and smiling like the happiest people on earth. Zac and Hilary are holding a trophy, kissing. The credits start to roll, but the first thing that pops up reads, "A Kidz Production!" Abby and I share a look of dread as the logo slowly rolls up the screen.

The lights come on, and EJ's mouth is all red and swollen like he's been assaulted by a vacuum cleaner. He has lipstick all over his face, neck, and ears.

"Jeez, Nicky, did you reapply?" Abby asks, handing EJ a Kleenex.

Parents with strollers are glaring at us as they walk out because of the lewd acts that were performed in our row. EJ still looks kind of lost as we step out of the theater. He points to a poster and suggests, "Yo, we should see *Fart Knockers* next!"

"No, we shouldn't," Nicky declares. "I have got to see *Cheer!* again!"

EJ's eyes sadly lower, and I smile. Abby tells them that they're on their own. "I need to see something smart, or my brain will fall out."

"Yeah, good call," I say as if I'm worried about my brain too.

5. THE ROCKET SHIP QUESTION

Waiting in line at the snack bar, Abby summarizes the article I was supposed to read about C. B. Down's film, *Genoa Eyes*. I think she was saying something about how rare it is for a first-time director to win the Cannes Film Festival, but she put her hand inside the back pocket of my Levi's as she was explaining it all, so I got a little sidetracked. Anyway, she paid for popcorn, Cherry Coke, and Milk Duds for our next screening. How awesome is she?

We casually stroll into the empty theater, and I ask, "Are you sure we got the time right?"

But the lights dim a few seconds later and the opening credits say, "Written and directed by C. B. Down." How cool is that? A guy that I've been in the same room with! A guy that went to my high school and saw me perform in the spring play . . . wrote and directed the most boring movie of all time! Oh my God. Most of it is in French or Russian, but they don't type out what's being said like they do in the other foreign movies that Abby has dragged me to. Ten minutes into the story, and I have a pretty good idea why we're alone. Abby must have misread the article, because the only award this thing should have won was the Trash Can Film Festival. I wonder if she told me how bad this movie was going to SUCK when I was spacing off in the snack bar line. The only thing more depressing than the violin music that plays over everything . . . is the nonexistent story line. It starts out with a guy shooting up on the bathroom floor of a crack motel in some foreign country. Then it flashes back to a time before his life was so screwed up and he had a hot girlfriend, but she only speaks Russian . . . or French (whatever they speak in the Bourne movies) so all they can do is have angry sex. Which would be awesome if they actually showed anything. This movie is going to give art films a bad name because you only see the action for a second or two before they cut to a shadow on the wall or a bird in the windowsill or something. He gets drunk a lot, chain-smokes cigarettes, and out of nowhere . . . she leaves him and joins the circus! He tries to find her but doesn't speak the Bourne language, and he doesn't seem to know where he is, so he can't find her. Then he goes back to the motel, and I think it turns out he's been dead the whole time. Roll credits! Awesome movie; where do they give out the awards?

I only *think* the guy died, because after watching this non-entertainment for two hours and twenty-three minutes, a guy taps me on the shoulder, shines his flashlight in my eyes, and asks to see our tickets.

I look over at him with my mangled left eye and bark, "You gotta be kiddin' me!"

He's startled by my appearance and stumbles backward before mumbling, "W-w-we didn't sell any tickets for this movie, so you obviously don't have them."

I jump up like I've been paroled from jail on a false arrest and ask, "Where the hell were you two hours ago with your ticket-sales info and flashlight?!"

"Sir, you have to go."

"We're gone," I say as Abby grabs my hand, and we walk up the aisle.

I can tell Abby is pissed, too, because she squeezes my hand and sounds like a frog when she mutters, "Unbelievable!"

We step outside the theater, and I see that she really is crying, so I instinctively give her a hug and say, "It's okay, it's finally over."

Her face is pressed into my collarbone when she asks, "Are you kidding?"

"Yeah, I'm joking. . . . It's probably gonna keep going for another hour or two."

She laughs. "Oh, for a second I thought that you didn't like the movie."

"Nooo, why would you think that? Who would *not* like it? I friggin' hated that movie."

She pulls back and asks, "Wait, are you kidding?"

"I do joke a lot, but I'm dead serious when I tell you that I'd like a two-hour refund on my life."

Her face is a combination of shock and disgust that I'd only expect to see if she were watching me eat a hot dog out of the trash. "You are so immature," she scoffs as she marches toward the ticket window.

Immature? Where the hell did that come from? I follow her to the box office, where she demands a student ticket for the next showing.

Genoa Eyes is rated R, so I make eye contact with the ticket guy and shake my head—"No"—flash ten fingers, then five, point to Abby, and mouth the words, "She's FIFTEEN!"

He asks to see her ID, and she flips around too fast for

me to drop my hands, so I shake both of them around and say, "Jazz hands!"

She doesn't laugh, so I try, "There goes their last chance to sell a ticket for that stinker. W-w-what do you want to do now?"

Her eyes narrow, and she storms off through the parking lot. I rush to unlock my bike, but stop to laugh when I see EJ's BMX still secured to the rack. I know that poor bastard is stuck in there watching *Cheer! The Musical* for the third time.

I roll up behind Abby, thinking about how I could seem more mature real quick, but she's wearing short shorts and taking really big steps. Her thighs are really strong, and they're jiggling provocatively as they rub together. . . . Anything intelligent I was thinking was just deleted. I don't even know where I am. I'm sure I was brewing up something super insightful that would make her forget about why she's mad at me, but maybe not. She's certainly striding away from me . . . kind of strutting, actually. Her booty is bouncing to a beat that makes me want to dance! *Boom, boom, boom, boom.* That damn "Go! Fight! Win!" song is burned into my brain, and it's burrowing into my loins, so I ride up beside her and bump her butt with my hip. I take my hands off the handlebars and start to ride circles around her. I clap my hands three times before cheering, "Y'all ready? OKAY! Let's GOOOO! Fight! Win. . . !" (*Clap clap.*) "Say it a-gain! And then we GOOOO! Fight! Win! Until we . . ." (I don't remember the words.) "Something, Gooo! Fight! Weeeeiiiaaaaaauuuuuueeeeeiiiiaana again!"

From behind I see her back shaking, so I pull up to confirm that she's laughing and not crying from embarrassment.

I keep riding, hands free, and act out the cheer/dance/clap routine as best I can. "Ready fo' a show, let's GO! With all ya might, let's FIGHT! That's the end and we WIN—"

Abby sings with me, "Until we Go! Fight! Win . . . again!" She jumps into the air and does the splits like it's no big deal.

"Wow, nice herkie!" I laugh.

"How do you know what a herkie is?" she asks.

"Oh, I was forced to sit through an entire movie about cheerleading one time."

She smiles.

"I'm sorry I didn't like your movie," I say seriously.

"No, I was upset and blew it out of proportion. I'm on my period so I'm all emotional."

Uhhh, we have officially taken a step . . . a personal step, a gross step, one I could have done without, but *I* am able to have conversations about many different subjects and want to prove that I'm not so immature after all. I try not to make a face as I add, "Oh, I-I-I know all about periods and tampons and PMSD. My dad refers to my sister's periods as 'exclamation points.'"

She, too, seems uncomfortable with our current topic. She raises her eyebrows and says, "That's a good story, Carter."

After an awkward moment we bust out laughing, and she finally hops on my axle pegs for a ride home. I think we're back on track so I divert our course through Merrian Park. The sun is going down and the huge park is almost deserted as she attempts to explain why she liked C. B. Down's award-winning/terrible movie.

"They weren't in a foreign country. . . . The language

barrier was just a metaphor. He'd lost his ability to communicate."

A lightbulb goes off in my mind, and I'm glad Abby is riding behind me and can't see it. She is so much smarter than me! "So he was just losing his mind throughout the story? I get it, but I'm still not entertained by it. I wouldn't see *Cheer! The Musical* again if you paid me, but it was at least amusing."

She asks, "Could you believe Hilary Idaho's boobs?"

"Yeah, where did those come from?"

"The silicone valley," she replies judgmentally.

"You think they're fake?" I ask, and offer up a reverse high five for the quick boob joke.

She slaps my hand and says, "Totally! I read all about her surgery in *US Weekly*. She was completely flat in her last movie and then all the sudden she's a C cup? Come on!"

I don't have much to say about Hilary Idaho's movies, but I love the fact that Abby and I are discussing cup sizes. "Isn't she our age?"

Abby replies, "She's sixteen! What kind of message does that send to her fans?"

"Tits are important!"

She whacks the back of my head and says, "Exactly! It's ridiculous, dangerous, elitist and—"

"Totally awesome!"

She whacks me again because she thinks I'm joking, so I add, "You can't get too high-and-mighty with your boomin' natural rack back there."

She doesn't have a rebuttal for that one. She may not appreciate having her breasts used against her in an argument. I'd like to stay on this subject for as long as possible, so I try to clarify my position. "I might actually agree with you. I happen to have a love/hate relationship with boobs. I'd probably get a lot more done if you guys didn't have 'em, but then I think . . . would I even get up in the morning?"

She doesn't say anything again. I believe that's the typical reaction when someone says something super profound.

We're rolling past the duck pond when she starts telling drama camp stories. She tells me how much fun she's having and that two kids have already fallen into the orchestra pit (I'm not the only one). She's really into the "coolness and maturity" of the college drama majors. She mentions one of her coworkers in particular a few times. She tells me, "His name is Carter, like you," and how he's "super funny" and "totally smart," and how much I'd "love him." Which is odd because hearing about the guy, and the tone of her voice, makes me think that I would not even like him, and I might want to punch him in his face if I saw it. But I don't want to be one of those guys who's always accusing his girl of stuff and acting immature and picking fights, so I just quicken my pace instead. She tells me about all the plays this College Carter Dumbass has starred in and how Ms. McDougle was talking to him about trying out for *my* part in C. B. Down's movie. And how she's going to rehearse with him too.

My legs are burning as we fly past the picnic area. I pant, "I thought it was a high school movie."

She explains, "Yeah, but he's such a good actor that he can easily pull off being younger."

"Is he short?"

"No, he's a bit taller than you."

"You know I'm still growin', right?"

"Why are you going so fast?"

"I don't know. I just like to ride this way sometimes!"

I'm not jealous, I'm not that guy, and my legs are on fire, so I squeeze the brakes and skid to a stop. I'd like to change the subject off of this a-hole who's moving in on my girl, so I just turn around and look her in the eyes. As she steps off the pegs to yell at me for stopping too fast, I give her a hard kiss that shuts her up. She may think another Carter is cool, but she's *my* girl.

A bolt of lightning shoots through my body as my forgotten bruises collide with her open mouth. "Yeaow, awesome, cool!" I say, pulling away from the pain.

She asks, "What's the matter with you?"

She seems confused when I reply, "Nothin'. Y-Y-You wanna go down the rocket-ship slide?"

My face is hot from riding hard, so the embarrassment shouldn't be that obvious. My lips are throbbing with pain. I grab her hand as we stroll past the swing sets. I'm trying really hard to pay attention while Abby explains how all of this land was part of the Saur mansion until the nineteen sixties. She tells me why nothing ever gets fixed in this park. She thinks it's because the newer suburbs have sucked up all of the money, but that's part of why Merrian is perfect for shooting this movie; it looks the exact same way as when C. B. lived here.

The sun is almost gone as I set my bike down and we climb the rickety spiral stairs to the top of the old rocket-ship slide. I've been up here a thousand times but never noticed how beautiful the view was. The slide is on top of a hill that overlooks most of Merrian. It all seems pretty small from up here. You can see the top of the Saur mansion and my school and the pool. The streets make sense when you're this high, and I can just make out Grey Goose Lake in the distance. I feel stupid for thinking it was so far away and for getting lost going out there. Abby tells me that this revelation is called "perspective" and that sometimes stepping away from something can give you a better look at it. I had no idea Merrian was in a valley. I was always too busy catching my breath from sprinting up the stairs in order to beat my sister or EJ to the top. The slide is super fun, long, twisty, and fast as hell, so I was always a little dizzy and too stoked about sliding down again to worry about perspectives or topographical appreciation. Or maybe it's just that I've never been up here with Abby before.

We stare at each other for a while before I pull her close. Pain shoots through my face again as she feels the romantic situation and kisses me. Dang it. I pull back after a few seconds and look into her eyes. I'm begging her to stop with my gaze, but she must think those tears in my eyes are sexy, because she comes in for more. Whoever invented the phrase "love hurts" must have dealt with something like this. I pull away again and roll my head to the side. She kisses my neck, and I moan a sigh of relief like I'm a guy who's really into getting his neck slobbered on. I grab her boobs because they're there, and who wouldn't? We've already established that boob is cool, but I've yet to try for more since our breakup/blowup last fall. Going up her skirt in a movie theater caused an uproar that rocked my school with scandal and wrecked my life for months, but I'd do it all over again in a second! I hope this rocket ship's rusty bolts can hold it down, because Abby and I are commencing the launch sequence! I slide my hands down her torso and unbutton the top button of her shorts as she cleans out my eardrum. I pause to make sure a slap isn't on the way before I go after the zipper. I give it a nervous tug and am halfway home when she aborts the launch and gives a chop block to my trembling hand.

She whispers, "My period . . ." and rebuttons her shorts before kissing my swollen lips again.

The pain is twice as bad as all the blood in my body rushes back upward. Not enough of it made it to my brain, however, to stop me from stepping back and asking, "So, d-d-do you wanna give me a blow job, then?"

I knew it was a dumb question the second it came out, and I wince from the stupidity, but I can't take it back and I just can't handle any more kissing. Rumor has it (Nutt's brother, Bart) that when a girl's on her period she's more likely to throw down a bj, for some reason. And Bart's (second-best) method to get a girl to give you one is to simply, "Ask for it." Abby looks out over the railing at the last moments of dusk and takes a deep breath. She may be drinking in the romance and thinking about how nice it would be for me to get my first blow job up here . . . and maybe what technique she should use. She's really thinking about it! This could be it . . . the best advice Bart has ever given. "Ask and ye shall receive!" She bites her lip, and I see tears welling up in her eyes. Dang it! My shoulders drop along with my face, spirit, and everything else.

In silence, she turns and walks down the stairs with heavy steps. I look down at the mulch-covered ground and think about throwing myself off. What a dumbass! I'm mortified at what I've just done, so I slide down to apologize. On accident, and out of pure instinctual habit, I squeal,

"Whooo-hooo!" on the way down. I come in for a hundred-mile-an-hour landing, almost plowing into Abby, who's just getting there herself. She's shocked to see that I've beaten her down here, and surprised by how drunk I seem to have become. She blows past me, and I dizzily stumble toward her. "I-I-I'm sorry."

"What are you sorry for, Carter?" she snaps back, and keeps going.

"Uh . . . you know . . . that I made you cry?"

"You're not sorry you asked me to give you a blow job?" she seethes.

"Yeah, I-I-I'm sorry about that too."

She stops walking like she's thinking up something mean to say, so I beat her to the punch and dig myself in a little deeper. "You know, Bart told me to just shove your head toward my crotch, and you'd just start doin' it. But I thought that because of the romantic setting, and me respecting you and all . . . like I do . . . that I could get by with the second-best technique."

Her head twitches and she barks, "What?"

"Haven't you ever heard, 'it never hurts to ask'?"

She marches off, and I grab my bike to give chase. When I catch up, she barks, "I'm not ready for all that and . . . and . . . you are so freaking immature!"

"That's the second time you've called me immature today."

"Well, you are."

This would be the perfect time to call her a bitch and assert myself as the alpha male, so in my own way, I do. "You're the one who's scared of a blow job!"

"So?" she asks defiantly.

I'm sure tonight or tomorrow I'll come up with a brilliant comeback to that question, but for now I just keep walking beside her and stewing.

She starts crying and then sobs, "Do you know how that makes me feel when you ask me something like that?"

I'm sure this is a trick question that I'm supposed to just think about, but I answer anyway. And I'm still trying to be a dick when I say, "Like my girlfriend, maybe?! Cuz that's what girlfriends do! I like hangin' out with you, but you're also really hot, and I don't want to just talk all the time."

"We were kissing—what's wrong with that? Why do you have to push?"

"I'm a guy, we push! And in case you aren't aware, this black-and-blue ball of bruise where my face used to be . . . friggin' hurts when you smash into it!"

She finally seems to get how jacked up I am and asks, "Why didn't you just say that?"

"I thought I did . . . by asking you to focus on other . . . uninjured areas!"

Logic! I said it with a mix of sass and hurt feelings. I'm the man! And she doesn't have any snappy comebacks either! She keeps walking in silence, though, until we reach the park's back gate. She finally stops and turns to me with tears streaming down her cheeks.

She looks pitiful when she says, "Stop. Don't walk with me anymore. I love you, Carter, but we just met too soon. We're the wrong people for each other at this point in our lives."

I have to laugh. "Oh my God! You're so dramatic!"

"And you're an immature asshole!" she bellows.

Dumbfoundedly, I ask, "Are you really breakin' up with me here?"

She just turns and sadly walks through the gates.

"Really?!" I demand. "I sat through those friggin' *Twilight* movies for you!"

She turns and barks, "But you didn't read the books like I asked you to!"

Unbelievable! She's just out of sight when I throw my bike as far as I can (about six feet). *How's that for mature, BI-ATCH?!*

6. WHO ORDERED A HOT DOG?

I wake up at the crack of ten fifteen a.m. the next day. I could barely get to sleep, but once I did, I went ahead and got nine and a half hours. Nevertheless, I'm rested, and I know what needs to be done. I've got to ride up to school and work out with my boys, and then immediately apologize to Abby. I throw on some shorts and a T-shirt, slam a protein shake, and tell my dad that I'll be back in about an hour to help him with the stupid deck. He took the day off of his real job to work on this junk, so he's fired up and tries to show me his drawings and explain why he's strung this yellow string all over the backyard, but I tell him I've got to get moving.

It's a perfect summer day. I've regained some of the feeling in my face, and I've got all of my lines memorized for the big audition—three days early! As soon as I knock out this apology, and Abby and I get back on track, this summer is going to be kicking ass!

Rolling into the parking lot, I see my boys' bikes locked up to various trees and signposts. Nick Brock's truck is parked next to the CRX, but my eye goes to the black Ferrari sitting in the back of the lot. It's beautiful and must be brand-new, because it has thirty-day tags. I bet they're getting personalized license plates made like 2FAST4U or

RCKTMAN! Who the hell got a Ferrari? If my football coach owns this baby, I may have to write a letter to someone, because he's overpaid! After gawking at it for a while, I lock up and am headed into the weight room when I hear the beat of a familiar song pumping inside the gymnasium. It's "Get Up Offa That Thing," by James Brown, and it's been stuck in my head for weeks because Abby's been working out a dance number to it. She's all stressed about it because it's her first chance to choreograph anything for the drill team. She's obviously the best dancer on the squad, and the older girls are pissed off about it, so they're making her audition this routine to see if she's got what it takes.

The gym door is propped open, so I slip inside. The drill team is facing the opposite direction, and they don't notice me. The number's going really well. I'm nodding to the beat and taking in the sights of a plus-sized dance troupe getting funky. They clap (almost in unison) and stomp a few times before swiveling their hips and leaping into a line. The girls touch the gym floor and slowly rise back up like a tsunami wave of purple sateen. Abby shimmies her boobs around, and they run toward half court. This must be the big finish. But I may see a problem. Two girls are headed for the same tape mark on the floor and they don't spot each other until it's too late . . . yep, problem . . . *SMACK!* They crash into each other, hard, before taking out a folding-chair prop and crashing to the hardwood dramatically.

I fight off the laughter because Abby seems disappointed and the music has faded out.

I think about clapping, but don't want them to think that I'm making fun, when I hear Nutt's voice boom from behind, "Who ordered a hot dog?!"

The entire drill team glances over their shoulders as a pair of hands slam into my hips, and I instantly regret two things at once:

A) Not tying the drawstring on my shorts.

B) Not taking the time to put on underwear this morning.

In a flash, my pants are around my ankles and my cheeks are as red as fire trucks . . . both sets! In front of me, the girls squeal with prude horror, and behind me, my boys howl with laughter as I stumble around, flapping in the breeze and frantically yanking my shorts back up.

I decide to put off the apology and chase my boys out the doors and around the parking lot, yelling, "Assholes!"

I stop chasing them after a few minutes when I see the awesome car again and gasp, "Yo, who's Ferrari?"

Bag tells me, "It's that writer who came to school last year."

"C. B. Down?" I ask.

"Yeah, he's in there workin' out with Bart and Nick Brock," EJ explains, just before I punch Nutt in the chest, and everyone groans their admiration.

Bag smiles mischievously and says, "Hey, Carter, do you need anything?"

I know he's messing with me, but I'm not sure what he's getting at, so I play along. "Nooo, why?"

Hormone chimes in. "You're sure we can't get you somethin'?"

I just stare at them until EJ yells, "You don't want a blow job this morning?!"

Son of a bitch! I punch Nutt in the chest again.

"OW!" he squeals. "It's not my fault you and Abby broke up!"

"Who the hell told you that?"

Doc explains, "EJ's bitch is here, and she was just yappin' about it."

EJ throws up his hands and protests, "Dude!?"

I shake my head in disgust. Why would Abby tell Nicky anything? I'm sure that she didn't mean for her to blab it to everyone, but still.

Still rubbing his boob like a bitch, Nutt continues, "Do not apologize to her, Carter! Bart says that she's just testing to see if you're a punk. If you grovel, she owns you, but if you man up and never speak to her again, you'll be hittin' it in a week."

I look around the group to see if what he said makes sense to anyone else. They all seem to be in agreement, so I decide to hold off on the apology, and we head into the weight room.

The old box fans are blowing hot air, and hard rock is blasting through the old speakers. The pool doesn't open until tomorrow, so everyone is here. The fine-ass Merrian Pool lifeguards are in here toning up for the big day. Bag's sister, Pam, and her gorgeous friend Jemma are wearing very short shorts and doing leg presses, so Nutt and I are getting warmed up next to the leg press today. He's bent over, squinting between his legs and hoping to catch a peek, but I can't stop gawking at C. B. Down doing pull-ups. You wouldn't think a writer would need to be in very good shape, but nobody told this guy. He grunts and snarls as he yanks his chin above the bar over and over again. His tattoos are bulging and glistening under the florescent lights.

I'm getting a drink of water when he walks up behind me and gasps, "S'up, Carter."

I turn in shock and mutter, "Hey, Mr. D-Down. I-I-I really enjoyed your book!"

He says thanks and gets a drink as I yammer on like a junior-high-school girl. "I mean, it was miserable, you know, but it's fun to read because it's not happening to me, you know? The script isn't nearly as good, though, you know?" *Of course he doesn't know—he wrote it! Shut up!*

He looks like he's going to rip my head off, but he doesn't. He nods and replies, "Yeah, that's what you get when you work with a committee. Try to please too many people, you wind up not pleasing anyone."

My favorite writer just shared something deeply personal with me, so I brilliantly point to the tattoo on his shoulder and ask, "D-D-Did that hurt?"

He continues, "I still believe that the heart of my story is in that script, and with the right actors, it's gonna be great."

Suspiciously, I ask, "You sold out to the Kidz Channel, right?"

His jaw flexes and the hawk tattooed on his neck cocks its beak at me in anger. "I didn't sell out to anybody, man. Kidz Channel is just one of the investors. . . . The higher your budget, the more freedom you have to—"

My face hurts from embarrassed contortion as I interrupt him, "No man . . . I uh, I'm not trying to put you down, I just saw the Ferrari out there, and . . . I think it's badass . . . I'm just not great at conversation."

He asks what happened to my face, and I explain the whole wreck and how gearing up to audition for his film is partly to blame for my wounds. He likes the cuts and bruises. He thinks they give me more "edge." He also tells me how much he liked my portrayal of Sky Masterson in *Guys and Dolls* and how he saw the show in London and preferred what I did over a professional actor! I finally stop grinning like an idiot when he asks if Abby and I are coming to the audition together.

"Yeah, no, we're fighting right now, because—"

His laughter interrupts me. "Oh yeah, your rocket-ship question? I heard about that."

Dang it! I try to change the subject. "You know, I've already got the audition scene memorized."

He takes a deep breath and nods a few times. He pulls at his beard and asks a fitness question. "Are you warmed up?"

I nod and he asks, "You wanna do some CrossFit?"

What am I gonna do, say no? But for those of you who don't know, if someone asks if "you wanna do some CrossFit," DON'T do it . . . it's awful! Within five minutes I'm ready to puke. As far as I can tell, it's this fitness program designed by the devil himself. It strings together a bunch of different exercises that all seem easy, but when you combine them, in order, it's like a painful-death simulator. You try to get your heart as close to exploding without actually allowing it the relief of combustion. It's a tantric heart attack. I'm lifting the same weight as Nick Brock and Paul Skelton, a.k.a. the Skeleton . . . This is not right! I've done more push-ups in twenty minutes than I've done in my whole life. C. B. is a madman.

He's totally exhausted from doing power cleans when I hear him snarl, "Sell out . . ." and then he does two more. I was doing push-ups at the time (go figure) and looking around for a trash can to vomit into when he said it, so I did five more and went immediately into squats . . . just trying to look busy.

As I'm hobbling across the parking lot to see if Abby has finished practice, C. B. walks up behind me and gasps, "Nice work, man. Hey, I invited those lifeguard girls and a few of your friends to have lunch with me—do you want to join?"

"Why?"

He laughs at me for a second, then says, "Well, I guess I didn't have many friends when I lived here, and I never had any money to do anything nice for anyone, so I want to try to be the cool guy around here for a change."

I shrug and say, "Makes sense to me." The next thing I know I'm shutting the door/wing of a Ferrari and flying down Merrian Lane. I'm trying to read the tattooed letters on his knuckles. He's talking about the movie or the auditions. The left hand says **S-T-A-Y**, for sure, but he keeps using the right one to shift gears and gesture as he talks about "concentration" or something. We rip into the Chipotle parking lot, and he's laughing at something. I'm pretty sure his right hand just says **F-O-C-U** . . . but that doesn't make any sense.

C. B. interjects with his deep gravely voice. "Stay focused."

"Huh?" I ask. Dang it, I've known him for less than an hour, and he's already figured out that I'm a space case.

"'Stay Focused.' That's what's tattooed on my fists," he says, showing me the letters printed on his knuckles. I'm still looking at the **F-O-C-U** when he laughs and says, "It's a joke. You get it?"

"You didn't have the 'focus' to finish the whole thing?"

He nods before turning the Ferrari off, and puts his pointer finger sideways under his nose. He's got another tattoo of an old-timey mustache on the side of it.

I start laughing. "You're crazy, dude."

He agrees. "I thought you'd like that."

The doors rotate up, and we climb out.

C. B. leans against the car and says, "Hey, for the audition . . . it's great that you memorized the lines, but I don't want you to get locked into that script."

I glance around in hopes that someone will see me hanging out with this dude. We close the doors and he continues, "I really want you to keep it loose and show these producer dickheads how great you are. Just bring that chemistry you and Abby brought to *Guys and Dolls*. It's electric and raw, and the camera is going to eat it up. These Kidz Channel guys just have to see it and feel it . . . so they'll get off my ass about casting Hilary Idaho and Zac-Michael Wienus."

I try to make him feel better. "They were pretty good in *Cheer! The Musical*."

He seems even more agitated when he says, "That's the exact comparison I don't want."

"At least they haven't turned your story into a musical."

He squeezes his face with his hands and adds, "I just heard this morning that they're trying to write songs."

"What could they possibly sing about? Your book is one of the most depressing things ever written."

He nods his thanks and explains how in the novel, Chris has dreams about his family and Maggie, so they want to delve into a happy place for a while and add these singing fantasy sequences.

I think that sounds ridiculous, but what the hell do

I know, so I try to keep it positive. "It could work."

It takes a few more minutes for Nick Brock, Bart, Skeleton, Pam and her friends Jemma and Yasmine, plus my boys (EJ, Doc, Nutt, Bag, Hormone, Levi, J-Low), this d-bag Andre, and ten other dudes to show up and get out of their overstuffed cars. We strut into the restaurant, still dripping with CrossFit sweat. We order the crap out of the menu because C. B. is buying. Massive amounts of food cover seven tables. I ordered guacamole and chips with my tacos for the first time ever, because my dad "will not pay three goddamn dollars for some chips that they should give you for free!" and C. B. will. We have the whole restaurant to ourselves because we're so obnoxious and stinky. Either that, or everyone else eating lunch on a hot Monday afternoon really wants to sit on the patio. I've never had so much fun eating, and these chips are worth the money! C. B. is the coolest adult I've ever been around. If anyone tries to talk about his movie, he changes the subject and tells a joke or he asks us a question, and it seems like he's really interested in the answer, like we're not just a bunch of smelly, dumbass kids who don't have Ferraris. I didn't expect the writer of such a depressing book to be so entertaining.

I wish all high school parties went down at Chipotle!

7. VARIOUS TECHNIQUES

I'm in the back of Nick Brock's truck, trying to pick a bug out of my eye, because Pam is now occupying the Ferrari's passenger seat. We're all headed toward her and Bag's house for an impromptu party. Bag seems worried about his sister in the race car, and this bug seems to be drowning in my eye.

When the truck finally rumbles into the driveway, a full-fledged party has spontaneously erupted. I thought we'd just play some video games and hang out, but my sister is here, along with most of my school, and miraculously, some of them are already drunk. If the Red Cross were as organized as the party grapevine in Merrian, a lot of lives would be saved.

I lose my second game of Wii tennis and start dancing in the kitchen next to a bunch of senior girls. It's fun, but all I can think about is how mad Bag's mom is going to be when she gets home from work, and how I wish Abby were here. I really should have apologized to her this morning. I like to copy her moves when we dance, and I want to talk to her about C. B. and tell her about CrossFit. She would dig it. I want to tell her how much my "perspective" has changed. It's only been a day, but I already miss her. . . . My boys are right, I am whipped!

After a while C. B. leaves to buy more alcohol, and since

this isn't my first rodeo with high school kids and booze, I split before he gets back and learns the secret reason you're not supposed to buy beer for teens: We're assholes.

I watch the Ferrari tear off down the road, and grab my bike out of Nick's truck. I'm looking at my watch, trying to figure out how fast I need to ride in order to get back to school before drama camp lets out, when my sister steps out of the house and breaks my train of thought by yelling, "You better have a good excuse for what you did!"

Dang it! I look into her eyes and know that someone just tattled. "I kind of do, but I can see that you won't agree, so forget it."

She's glaring at me like I stole this bike from a blind kid. "You just think that you're sooo special because you're auditioning for this movie and hanging out with this writer, but if you think you can start treating the people who care about you like dirt, you're going to seriously regret it. Like you're Christian friggin' Bale all the sudden?!"

"Shut up! I don't think that, and I'm going to go apologize right now."

"Good! Regret is a decent place to start, but you need to *show* how sorry you are. You need to work extra hard to prove you're remorseful, and you'll be on your way to getting the things you want."

Is she telling me how to get Abby to put out more? Why is she using this weird, inspirational code language? That's not usually her style. "Okay, oracle, so if I'm not supposed to 'just ask for it,' how do I get her to give me a blow job?"

Her left eye snaps shut like she's just eaten a lemon, and her head cocks to the side. I don't think we're talking about the same thing.

I throw up my hands and say, "Wait! Let's start with what *you* think I should be sorry for."

She considers her next statement very carefully, tapping her lips with her index finger before seething, "I thought that you should be embarrassed that our father is sitting in the backyard with a broken heart and a pile of lumber because his only son is nowhere to be found. . . ."

Dang it, I totally forgot about him!

She continues. "But unless I'm mistaken . . . you're telling me that you've also asked Abby—the best girlfriend you're likely to ever have—to give you a . . . ahh . . . it's so disrespectful that I can't even bring myself to say it."

"Ah come on, you can too . . . BLOW JOB! It was just a question—I didn't throw her off the rocket-ship slide. It doesn't hurt to ask, and you're the one who told me to use questions in the first—"

Her face contorts even further as she barks, "Stop right there, idiot! I told you to ask questions about her, questions that would make her feel special . . . not degrade her! Do you know how that makes a girl feel?"

I obviously don't, so she continues, "Like a used object! Things like pushing a girl's head down into your crotch are techniques that guys use on girls that that they don't care about. I'm not telling you those things won't work on insecure skanks, because they do. There are moves you make on girls you respect, and they are different than the ones you use on girls you DON'T. Trust me, *we* know the difference! Pity the boy who thinks he has control. Girls of quality will do these things if and when *we* want to . . . or we won't. All you can really do is get us *not* to do things. And the best way to *not* get a cool chick to do something . . . is to push her."

I drop my head onto my handlebars in frustration. She pats my back and says, "Now, don't beat yourself up, you made a mistake, but you're lucky enough to have me pointing these things out for you. You're learning the hard way, but you're learning. Now, get over to her house and apologize, and then go home and help dad with that deck!"

I raise my head and ask, "Why can't you help him?"

"Because I'm a girl and—"

"Yes, I'd like a double standard with cheese, please. . . ."

"And he didn't ask me . . . He wants to bond with your dumb ass for some reason."

She heads back into the house, and I hear her bark at EJ, "Get off the table, idiot!" He's spent so much time at our house that she feels obligated to straighten him out too. I think she reserves the more heartfelt tips for me, though. He just gets yelled at.

I pass the liquor store on Merrian Lane and wave to C. B. as he's loading the Ferrari with beer. He seems puzzled as to why I'm on the road, so I wave a kind of pre-apology for what my friends are about to do. He just gives me a nod.

Drama camp has probably let out, and I'm closer to Abby's house than school, so I bust a left onto her street. I wonder if she's already forgiven me and is walking toward my house right now so that she can interrupt my dad's construction project and ask me to go up to the bedroom so we can "talk" privately. And she'll cry when I tell her how I confused her for a skank and how sorry I am and how I totally understand how she feels, and she'll apologize for blowing it out of proportion and telling Nicky about it, and then she'll slowly take off her clothes so that we can have make-up sex and there will be sunlight streaming into my windows so that I can clearly see her—

"Whoooa!!!" I yell when I realize I'm riding through Abby's yard and have just crushed a bush and row of flowers. I slam on the brakes and swerve to miss the mailbox before finally skidding to a stop. I look over my shoulder and lock eyes with Abby's pissed-off mother . . . who was about to trim the bush I assassinated. I can see that she doesn't appreciate the fact that I just saved her some work, and that she wouldn't mind putting those clippers in her hand to use on me.

"Sorry," I yell, looking at the missing swatch of grass.

She looks at my back tire for an explanation and asks, "Can I help you?"

"Uhhhh, is Abby around?"

She tells me that she's still at drama camp and continues to glare at me. I nervously mutter, "S-S-She's probably rehearsing for the audition, huh?"

She explains, "No, Abby isn't planning to audition anymore."

"What? Why?"

"She doesn't want to be in the same room with you."

I'm able to ignore her snotty tone because I'm so pissed about the fact that Abby might not do something that she really wants to because of me. This may be her only chance to audition for a movie, and she'll regret it forever if she doesn't, so I tell her mom very seriously, "You should make her."

She pointedly replies, "I don't *make* Abby do anything, Carter."

I look away and think about defending myself with

an explanation of the various techniques one might utilize when trying to elicit a blow job, and how I actually chose the method with the least amount of pressure, but I just let the guilt hang there until she sadly says, "You should be nicer to her."

I look down at the skid mark in her yard and think about what other damage I may have caused around this house in the past year. I don't give any excuses. I just sigh, "I know," and pedal off.

I lean my bike against the brick wall of the drama department and walk inside. The usually deafening hallway is now a ghost town. The sound of Abby's laughter floats out of the little theater and makes me smile. She may not be in such a bad mood after all. I'm making my way through the backstage curtains when a guy's deep voice stops me in my tracks and sends a chill down my spine. I peek through the black cloth to find her and a lanky college guy sitting on the steps of the theater, drinking Diet Cokes. He's definitely a drama nerd, but cooler than most of the ones around here. His hair is perfectly sticking up all over the place like a Wienus Bro, and he's leaning back on his elbows while his long legs dangle into the orchestra pit. Abby is sitting with her arms wrapped around her knees, looking at him like he's a movie star telling a fantastical tale.

"So, it's opening night," he bellows. "It's just a college show, but everyone else is nervous because they're all terrified of Shakespeare. I'm backstage, changing my costume, when this little freshman—no offense to you, Abby—comes running up to me screaming, 'Carter, you're on! You're on!'"

Hold up! This is Carter? I bet it's his first name. Carter

is a d-bag name, unless it's your last name and people just call you that.

He continues telling his lame theater story, in his nasally monotone voice, about how someone forgot their lines and he saved the day. I think I fall asleep for a minute, but he finally wraps it up by saying, "The Duke walks past me again, I grab his leg and yell, 'The king *really* entreats your patience, good sir!'"

Abby laughs. "That was brilliant!"

Nooo, it wasn't! I could think of a hundred better ways to make that screwup work. I'm just about to step out there and break off one of my own funny theater stories, when Abby says, "Oh my God, my ex-boyfriend was always putting Jeremy and me into those situations. This one time, during *Guys and Dolls* dress rehearsal . . ."

My brain shorts out for a second and my head twitches. *Ex-boyfriend? Like, me, ex-boyfriend?* And I'm not positive of this because I can't hear very well with this steam shooting out of my ears, but I believe she just made fun of me! Okay, okay . . . I'm not going to freak out . . . and I'm not going to cry . . . very much! But tears are streaming down my cheeks, and I'm as pissed off that she's causing me to cry as I am to be the butt of her damn joke. I wipe the water off my face and bolt for the parking lot.

I fling the door to the drama department open and step out into the light as Ms. McDougle pulls into the parking lot. I grab my bike like it owes me money, but the handlebars catch on my gym shorts and rip them open at the crotch, so I shove the bars back the other way. They bounce off the wall and smash into my bare balls . . . really hard.

"Ohhh!" I gasp, and double over with pain.

Ms. McDougle yells, "Carter! Are you okay?"

"Dang iiitttt! NO!" I cry into the grass, and try not to flash her my wounded junk. "Not even close!"

"What's going on?" she asks.

"W-W-Why don't you ask your other Carter Casanova College Dumbass in there?!" I yell, and punch the brick wall. "OWWWW!!!" Man, I *am* immature.

"What are you talking about?" she says with great concern. "Was he doing something to Abby?"

"NO, she was doing something to him, though . . . and me!" I'm crying again.

"What did she do to him?" Ms. McDougle demands.

"She, s-s-she made fun of me," I mutter.

She sighs. "Oh good . . . Not good for you, of course. I just overheard Abby telling him the other day that she was a freshman in college and—"

"So she's been flirting with him this whole time?!"

I don't wait for an answer. I just pull my shirt down to cover my exposed nards and hop on my bike before blasting through the streets of Merrian. My poor body has been wrung out today, but I drive the pedals as hard as I can. This bike and body are all I've got to take out my frustrations on.

8. CHEERLEADING SKIRT

The next day I'm way too sore to even think about helping
with the stupid deck, but I don't have the heart to bail on
my dad again. He's taken another day off of work and is giving me the most pitiful look when I come downstairs. So I
get to dig postholes all day and mix concrete with a shovel,
yeah! Oh my God, it sucks soooo bad, but it gives me the
chance to think about my audition scene and brood over all
the ways I might get to yell at Abby. Even if she doesn't
show up and I get paired with another actress, I'll still put
Abby's face on her body and bitch her out so bad she won't
know what hit her. Before I know it, the day is over, and
my dad hands me eighty bucks. My fingers don't work after
gripping that shovel all day, so I have to take the bills with
both hands. I'd like to tell him, "I don't want your money,
Father! Getting to spend the day with you was pleasure
enough for me!" I know that's what he wants to hear, but I
just can't do it. Instead, I shove the twenties into my dirty
pocket and stumble inside.

Flipping through the channels on the basement TV, I stop
to watch a Wienus Bros concert for a while (mostly because
the remote sucks down here and won't change channels, but
I'm also interested in Zac-Michael now that he's trying to

steal my part in *Down Gets Out*). I want to hate him, but he seems to be having so much fun and his hair is so awesome that I just wish I was him. How much ass would it kick if performing were your job? You just get up at noon and go sing and jump around a stage like a dork for screaming girls. You might not have to lift eighty-pound bags of concrete that burn your skin and hurt your back even more than CrossFit. And your dad wouldn't call you a wuss when you pour the bags into the wheelbarrow too fast and run away from the toxic dust screaming because it's, no doubt, mixing with the moisture in your lungs and trying to make a statue out of you. How's that for Dickens?!

It must be a "Wienus-athon," because Hilary Idaho pops onto the screen after the song finishes and yells, "ALRIGHT! Let's give it up for the baddest brothers on Kidz! Check out my new video, 'Go! Fight! Win!' from *Cheer! The Musical*, in theaters now! Let me know what you think! Log onto Kidzchannel.net and post a review, homies!"

The old remote decides that I need to watch her video, too, and I don't have the energy to get up and change the channel, so I take a deep, painful breath (partly because of Abby and what happened after we saw this movie, but mostly from sore stomach muscles) and watch. It's a lot of *Cheer! The Musical* footage but then a bunch of stuff with just Hilary dancing and shaking her new boobs. She raps in the video, which is just wrong, but her dance moves are on the money.

I lean closer to the screen (ouch) to see if her boobs are really fake or not. I need a friggin' pause button. She sings, "The ice you're on, sucka, is awful thin . . . We gonna GO! FIGHT! WEEEIIIIIAAAAHHHEEEEENNA!!!" She has the black stuff under her eyes like she's a football player, and she keeps crawling across the field like a cat. It's pretty sweet, actually.

I hear someone coming down the stairs, but the remote will not help me out. EJ bounds into the room, lifts his shirt, and swivels his hips around before yelling with Hilary on the TV, "Your team ain't nothin' but a has-been! GO! FIGHT! WEEEIIIIIAAAAHHHEEEEENNA!!!"

I have to laugh, and it hurts so bad, but he's jumping all around, kicking and cheering, "Who, who, who's the gayest kid I know?!"

I don't say anything, so he repeats, "I said, Who, who, who's the gayest kid I know?!"

I shake my head and mutter, "Who?"

"Give me a C!"

I mumble, "C."

"Give me an A!"

"A."

"Give me an R!"

I say, "Easy fella, you're the one who memorized the words and dance moves!"

He replies, "How can you not? It's the most annoying song ever! I've seen the stupid movie five times! I'm not even here to see you. I came to borrow a hammer from your dad to try to beat this tune out of my brain."

"Stop making me laugh, dude. It hurts."

"Come on, everyone is waiting for us in the CRX. There's a party by Merrian Park."

I tell him that I can't go, and he calls me lame, but I need to study for the audition (and I kind of hate parties).

"You were watchin' porn before I came down, weren't you?"

"No, just Hilary Idaho."

"That'll do. She's hot!"

"You know her boobies aren't real?" I ask.

"Nuh-uh!" he declares. "Are they CGI?"

"Just silicone, I think."

"Bart says that you don't want to squeeze 'em too hard 'cause they can pop."

"I'll keep that in mind."

Then he starts humping the air in front of him to the beat of the music and says, "Yo, Nicky put on her cheerleading skirt and nothing else, and we . . ."

"STOP!!! Aren't the guys waiting for you?"

He runs for the stairs, saying, "Oh crap!" But then he comes back into the room and asks, "So that's it for you and Abby, huh?"

"That's it for me. She was flirtin' with some college guy all week . . . and she made fun of me to entertain him."

"Abby was talking to Nicky at the pool this afternoon, and I guess the drama teacher told her that you were cryin' in the parking lot, so she knows."

I throw up my hands. "I racked myself! I wasn't crying about—"

EJ interrupts me. "Whatever, dude. You cry at Hallmark commercials. She seems pissed at you for spyin' on her, but I don't even think she likes that dude. Nicky told me not to tell you, but why the hell would Abby talk to Nicky in front of me if I wasn't supposed to report it to you?"

I shrug my shoulders like I don't know or care, but that info does make me feel better. EJ advises me to not talk to her for a while. To allow her to miss me so much that she goes crazy and comes over with a cheerleading skirt on. He also thinks that we should TP her house, but that doesn't seem right (deforestation and all). He's setting up the video game player when I remind him of the five dudes stuffed in the CRX. He sprints up the stairs, singing, "Go! Fight! Win!"

ADD is easier to spot in other people . . . and much funnier.

9. AUDITION

I ride up to school extra slow so I'm not sweating too bad for the audition, but my heart starts pounding when I see the Ferrari in the parking lot. I turn into a fountain of perspiration when Abby's mom's minivan pulls into the circle drive behind me. I look away because for some damn reason, I'm smiling! I guess I'm happy that Abby decided to show up, but I'm still pissed at her. How can I expect to cry on cue if I can't stop myself from smiling? I lock up my bike and try to stroll into the school as if I didn't notice her.

There's a different vibe here than there was at the *Guys and Dolls* tryouts. Everyone is still nervous, but no one is running around singing or laughing for no reason. About ten kids are politely sitting in folding chairs outside the auditorium. I write my name on a list and look over at Abby's College Carter Dumbass reading over the same scene I'm about to audition for. Dang it! He's going to get the part for sure. He's got all this experience and funny theater stories, and his hair is perfect. How am I supposed to compete with a college drama major? He looks up from his script and catches me staring at him.

I try to play it off by muttering, "I'm gonna go fix my hair," and strut toward the bathroom. Abby walks by, and we pretend not to notice one another. Dang it! I slam the door and give myself a disappointed look in the mirror. My face is so jacked up, I'm sweating, my cheeks are all red, and my hair is so boring! Why am I even here? This is a waste of time. They're going to cast a Wienus Brother, and if they can't get one, they'll give it to somebody with a better stylist and more experience. I couldn't be confused for a pretty boy by a blind person since the bike wreck, and I've only done one play . . . which Abby said I was always screwing up, and you don't go from wrecking the spring musical to starring in a movie—

"STOP IT!!!" I yell into the mirror. *Stop sabotaging me!* C. B. thinks I'm great; I just need to show them and spike my hair a little bit. But it looks ridiculous when I do, so I get it wet and try to slick it to the side. That looks retarded, so I stick my head under the hand dryer until I look like a scarecrow (hit by lightning).

"Seriously, STOP IT!!!" I shout again. This just didn't feel real until now. Like I was dreaming that they're shooting a real film in Merrian and I have a chance to be in it. . . . It's probably hard for anyone to believe that dreams come true, but here I am. I take a few deep breaths and try to shake the nerves off. *Don't be scared.* C. B. is just a guy from Merrian who drives a race car and thinks Ms. McDougle is cool. I thrash around for a second and scream, "Do it!"

When I rush out of the crapper, I almost run into Jeremy.

"Haaaa!" he cries. "Carter, what the hell happened?"

"Oh, I wrecked my bike."

He clarifies, "No, I mean, what happened to your hair?"

I shake my head, like I don't want to talk about it. He tries in vain to fix it as Ms. McDougle emerges from the auditorium and reads from her clipboard. "Carter and Sarah, you're up."

My heart starts to pound and a sweat bead runs into my eye. Luckily, College Carter Dumbass gets up like it's his turn, and I've got a few more minutes to try and pull myself together. Unluckily, he bends down and kisses Abby on the cheek before going into the theater. Shock like a lightning bolt shoots down my spine. Abby catches me watching the exchange, turns red, and retreats to the girls' bathroom. On top of my other issues, I've started to cry, so I dart for the safety of the boys' bathroom again. I am such a bitch, and my hair is so jacked! This could be the biggest day of my life, and Abby is screwing me all up! I can't let her do this. Please get it together, and breathe! I beat my head against the wall for a while and start to forget my troubles, but head trauma is a flawed way to deal with your problems, because I also start to forget who I am. I plop down on the toilet and squeeze my skull in between my hands and rock back and forth for a few minutes. I'm starting to regain my senses and feel a little better when McDougle knocks on the door and asks, "Carter?"

"Uhhh, yes?"

She tells me I'm up, so I blow my nose and run out into the hall. The other kids are staring at me as I jog into the auditorium. I'm looking down at my script when I enter the dark room. I'm not really reading; I'm just trying to look busy. I glance up and see Ms. McDougle smiling at me with C. B. Down and a group of guys wearing sport coats. They all have headsets blinking in their ears. It's way too hot outside to be wearing any kind of coat, so these dudes must be important.

McDougle's smile makes me feel better for a second, and then it all comes crashing down when I see Abby awkwardly standing off to the side of the stage, waiting. Dang it.

I step into the light, as far away from her as possible. She's supposed to be wearing a prom getup, not a cute yellow dress that displays her cleavage. FOCUS! McDougle breaks the silence by saying, "Okay, you two? Abby and Carter, this is C. B. Down, Phil Coates, and the rest of the *Down Gets Out* production team."

I give them a nod, and Abby mumbles, "Nice to meet you."

Now I feel like I have to say something, so I do. "Nice sport coats."

I didn't even realize I'd said anything until I see the shock on McDougle's face and C. B. laughing. The guy next to him clears his throat and says, "Phil . . . it's Phil Coates. . . . Did you have a question?"

I'm still looking at Abby, who's staring at the floor. "No, I'm good, let's get this over with."

McDougle cringes. "Carter?!"

Abby approaches and whispers in my ear, "Are you okay?" with real concern.

I reply softly into her ear, "Yeah, I think I'm just being 'immature' or something. . . . I'm sure I'll get over it." She pushes off me, and I tell the casting group, "We're ready!"

C. B. smiles and says, "All right, you guys have read the script? Scene thirty-four, at Maggie's house. Start with Chris yelling the line, 'I can't believe you'd do this to me!' Okay?"

I shrug and take a deep breath, looking at Abby with so much contempt and anger that I'm shaking. I don't yell the line, in fact I barely open my mouth when I quietly seethe, "'I cannot believe you'd do this to me.'"

She knows I'm talking directly to her, and she just stares at me for a second. As written, she's supposed to be "embarrassed" before she gets "angry," but she skips straight to the anger. Abby gives me another shove and barks, "'WHAT?! What have I done to you, Chris? Other than love you?!'"

The only moment it wasn't *Abby* yelling at *me* is when she called me "Chris." Her words hang in the air, because for some reason I've decided that this would be a good time to cry again. This isn't the crying part of the scene, so I'm fighting back tears as I try to say the next line. I'm supposed to call her a liar, but she doesn't allow me to get it out.

She scolds, "'I am the only person who cares about you, and you break my heart over and over again, because you're so selfish that you can't see how much I need!'"

I pull it together enough to say the next line. "'What? What the hell do you need? You have EVERYTHING. . . . You're popular and beautiful and rich—'"

She pushes me, hard, and knocks the pages out of my hand, so I start freestyling a bit. "Quit pushin' me!"

Abby's got mad improv skills, so she replies, "You need someone to push you, pussy," and shoves me again.

That seemed a little out of character for Maggie to say, but I roll with it and say, "Dude?!"

She tries to get us back into the dialogue when she says, "'Can't you see that none of this matters to me?'"

I don't need the script when I say the actual line, "'All I can *see* is that you're going on a date with someone other than me, and he's taking you somewhere I can't. You don't care about me. All the rest is just details, because you can't love something that you pity—'"

She's supposed to tell me, "That's not true!" but all I allow her to get out is "'That's—'" before I start going off on her. "'Don't deny it! It's all over your face since you caught me in that Dumpster!'"

Tears well up in her eyes, and she struggles to get the words out. "'I'm sorry.'"

I don't let up on her. I yell, "'I have to dig through trash to survive. I'm an animal, and you couldn't pretend anymore that I'm not!'"

She just sadly nods her head. Man, she's such a great actress and so beautiful, I hope more people can see her do this. Focus! I have to pick up the script and read, "'I'm sorry, too, because I'm getting out, and you're not.'"

She's really crying when she nods and mutters, "'Good . . . and you're right.'"

I say, "'I just can't give you anything—'"

She cuts me off and is totally frustrated with me when she yells, "'I don't want anything, Chris! You're just too much. I love to joke around and play make-believe, but you—'"

I feel a tear roll down my cheek as I say, "'The greatest moments of my life have been pretending with you.'"

She shakes her head and softly cries, "'I guess I need more than pretend.'"

I nod at her like I've got more to say, but the lines are over. The auditorium is dead silent. I knew I'd have to get mad during the scene, but that was intense. We look at each other, and I have to smile because I think that audition just went awesome! I love it when I have time to prepare. There just never seems to be enough time in regular life to be really prepared for anything.

I shield my eyes from the lights and peer out into the seats for a reaction. Maybe I was mumbling. That's the first thing McDougle usually tells me when I finish a scene. But they all have their heads down like they're asleep. Are they crying? Abby looks as confused as I am.

C. B. seems really upset and is shaking around. We may have done *too* good of a job. The lines just seemed to be written for Abby and me, but they were really about two other people, sitting ten feet away. That would be pretty intense to see some kids act out a scene from your life.

Phil Coates eventually stands and clears his throat before telling Ms. McDougle, "Okay, we've got to keep moving. Let's get the next kids in here."

C. B. jumps up and starts kicking the chair in front of him. McDougle hugs him to stop him from wrecking her new theater seats. They're both still crying, but he's cussing up a storm through his tears, and bellows, "It just throws it all up in my face! I have no control over this thing!"

McDougle responds, "No one has control."

He sobs, "You do. You've taught these kids for a year, and they're ten times better than anyone we saw in New York or LA, and it's gonna drive me crazy because I can see how good this film could be with these nobodies in the roles. . . ."

Hold up: did he just call Abby and me "nobodies"?

He points at the sport coats, screaming, "I sold it to them! It's theirs! I have to cast Hilary Idaho and that Wienus Brother . . . and once I do, they're going to destroy my story."

Phil is glaring at me like this is my fault.

Abby makes a face, points at the script, and mouths, "Hilary Idaho?"

I nod my head and cup some imaginary boobs on my chest to let Abby know what I think of that. She shakes her head in disgust, but I don't care—I'm being myself from here on.

C. B. finally says to the sport coats, "So, that's what I wanted you to see. We can stop this casting session right now. If you guys can't see how great these kids are . . . how much more honest that performance was than anything else we've seen . . . then you shouldn't be in the film industry."

Sport Coat Phil tugs at the lapels of his jacket and corrects him. "Sorry, C. B., but we actually make movies—hit movies. This session was just a publicity stunt to win over the locals, and it failed. The media didn't even show up, because without stars, no one cares. Yes, these kids were great, and maybe the story would come through in a more truthful way if we cast them, but who cares? This is a business, and my company has invested way too much time and money in Zac-Michael and Hilary not to give them great parts like these in a project that, frankly, would get completely ignored without bankable actors or great musical numbers."

I think about mentioning the other Kidz Channel sure-fire ingredient: the talking dog! But I keep it to myself. Sport Coat Phil asks Ms. McDougle to show in the next group and explains, "I'm trying to find actors for the smaller roles, so we don't have to fly anyone in, or pay people we don't have to."

C. B. yells, "You can't do this, asshole!"

"Yeah, I can. We own the rights to your story, and we can get a new director if we want to! But we won't, because you're cheap, and we think you'll do an interesting job. You could always return the money. . . . No, that's right, you spent it all!"

I shoot C. B. a thumbs-up in approval of his decision to buy a Ferrari. He fights off a smile because this is no time for jokes. Ms. McDougle ushers Abby and me out the door. When it closes, Abby covers her mouth and starts giggling. "Wow."

I offer up a high five and say, "No matter what happens, you should know that you were great."

She slaps my hand and replies, "Me? You were the next Daniel Day-Lewis in there."

That makes me smile because I know he's her favorite actor.

She adds, "That producer is a dick."

The entire waiting room is staring at us. College Carter Dumbass walks up, grabs Abby's hand, and asks, "What happened?"

I attempt to set their hands on fire with my stare before I bark, "Yo, we're havin' a conversation here," like a total dick. My mom says I'm "very impressionable," so watching C. B. go off in there may have rubbed off on me. Or I'm just a hardcore badass now, and everybody needs to get used to it.

Abby tells him, "Just give us a minute, please."

He looks pissed and replies, "Well, I have to go."

I shoot him a snarky nod as she grabs my arm and whispers intensely, "He's giving me a ride home, but it doesn't mean anything, okay? I'll call you later."

"I can take you home."

"No, my mom won't let me ride on your pegs any-more. . . ."

"Look, I understand what I did wrong. I treated you like a skank, but you're a quality girl, and there are different rules for getting girls of quality to put out—"

She makes a weird face and says, "I can't ride with you. I'll call you—"

I throw up my hands because I'm sick of this. I was trying to be cool, but I'm back to the prick technique when I bark, "You know what, save your minutes . . . because *my* mom won't let me talk to *you* anymore."

"What?"

"Yeah, she thinks that you're a bitch . . . and I'm pretty sure she's right."

Her mouth drops, and I'm on my toes in case she decides to take a swing, but tears fill her eyes and she nods her head before muttering, "Perfect then, a typically imma-ture reaction to a normal request."

"Normal request?" I retort. "You were my girlfriend last week, and you're about to get into a car with a guy I saw you flirting with and who thinks, because you told him, that you're in college!"

I tried to say it loud enough for College Carter Dumbass to hear. She storms off, muttering something about "con-text" and "immature jerk." He follows her out the door. I watch them drive off, and my stomach hurts because I know that I just missed an opportunity here, and I've got to get home and dig ten more postholes before filling them with concrete.

10. INSTINCTS

The next morning my dad and I are getting the tools out of the garage when he starts blathering, "Hopefully you're learning the value of a dollar here and getting a taste of manual labor . . . and you'll put a little more effort into your studies next year so you won't have to dig postholes for the rest of your life." He sips his coffee with parental satisfaction. It's barely nine a.m., and he's already annoying me.

At three o'clock my hands don't work anymore, and I've got white dust in my hair, eyes, and mouth, but the footings are finally done, and my dad gives me another eighty bucks. I offered to pay him eighty-five dollars not to make me work tomorrow, but he just laughed like I was kidding. It actually wasn't so terrible to hang out with him. We talked about my troubles with Abby, and he shared a story about a rough summer he went through, long before I was alive, when he dropped out of college and became a roofer. He was in love with some girl (I picture an eighties rocker chick with big hair who's into roofers), and she broke his heart (not so into roofers after all). He wasn't concentrating at work and fell off a twenty-foot ladder. His leg was broken, so he enrolled in summer school. He met my mom, who was a nerd that took summer school for fun. They hit it off, graduated, got married, moved to Merrian, and had two kids. . . .

I start snoring to make him think that his story is boring, but he shoots me with the water hose and sums up his point: "Some of the prettiest flowers grow in piles of crap."

I give him a nod to let him know that I get his point, because sometimes he thinks I'm still five years old. Or an idiot.

I'm cleaning out the wheelbarrow when a black Ferrari pulls into the driveway. *VROOOOMMM!!!* The door rotates up and C. B. springs out, much happier than the last time I saw him. "Carter, you're a mess!"

My dad comes around the house to see what's going on and to check out the car. They make small talk for a while before C. B. asks my dad, "Do you think you could spare him for a few weeks so that he can star in a movie with Hilary Idaho?"

I hear my crusty eyelids open from shock. My dad is super excited (after we explain who Hilary Idaho is). And I'm so happy that I don't have to build this damn deck anymore!

Dad asks him to stay for dinner, and we're both shocked when he accepts the invitation. But not half as alarmed as my mom is when she sees this tattooed badass walk into her kitchen. I'm not sure if she's worried about having enough food, or him killing us. C. B. seems so stoked to eat a home-cooked meal that my mom relaxes and can't help but start to mother him.

In between bites of turkey tetrazzini he goes over all the details. How my part was offered to Zac-Michael, but his agent/mother wanted so much money that it pissed off Sport Coat Phil. Then they tried to get the kid from *The*

Wiz Kidz Show, but they couldn't get him out of rehab in time. I assume there were a few more guys that fell through before I got the job, but C. B. spared us. And since they're so close to shooting, they decided the best thing to do was just give the part to a "nobody" . . . ME! And I am going to get paid. When Phil said that he didn't have to pay the locals, he meant, like, millions of dollars. I have to join some actors union, and after they take half of the money, I'll get, like, six hundred bucks a day! But my folks immediately start yapping about a 529 college savings plan, and I know that I'd actually have seen more of the deck money. I don't really care, because the word "jealous" doesn't begin to describe the look on Lynn's mug all through dinner. She's in a state of confused, angry shock until C. B. tells her that she can be a wardrobe stylist's assistant's assistant . . . if she joins their union.

He also plans to ask Abby to be Hilary Idaho's stand-in, but she'll have to join a union for stand-ins. Ms. McDougle is going to play the teacher who inspires my character and enters his writing in the scholarship contest.

Mom hesitantly asks, "Can you learn all the lines in a few days?"

"MOM!" I declare as maturely as I can.

C. B. explains, "It doesn't matter, we just do little bits at a time. You get an idea of the scene, then we have to block it out for the camera and lighting guys, and I want Carter to improvise a lot. Keep it loose and work off of that great instinct. We can fix or add the little details in post-production. Don't sweat the filming at all."

Man, does this not make sooo much sense?! I was born to be an actor. No homework, keep it loose? Use your instincts? I fail tests all the time because I don't get the details right, but I always get the ideas!

History: War is good.

Social Studies: War is bad.

Geography: Wars were fought here, here, and here.

Science: No one really knows anything, but these are the "laws" we've pulled out of our asses.

Stop wasting my time and let me use my instincts!

C. B. was saying something, but all I'm able to catch is, "Just go over to her hotel around noon on Monday."

"What? Who's hotel?" I ask.

"Hilary Idaho's," he says, like it was obvious. My family's shocked faces confirm my sentiment that it was anything but obvious.

"Really?" I ask.

C. B. continues, "Yeah, you'll try on costumes and get to know each other. It's real informal. I'm hoping that you can maybe help her try to act like a regular kid. She's got some issues. Anyway, just show her your world a little bit, but watch out for her bodyguard."

I nod like all of that sounded pretty normal, but my brain is flipping around my skull trying to figure out what I'm going to say to an international superstar. And how incredibly lame "my world" is going to seem to her. I'm not very cool around regular people—how the hell am I going to be around Hilary friggin' Idaho?

C. B. snaps his fingers in my face and says, "Stay focused, man." Then he clenches his fists and threatens me with his tattooed knuckles.

I instantly pop out of my daydream, and everyone is super quiet, staring at C. B. For the first time my dad isn't so sure he wants me hanging out with this guy. Either that or he's thinking about getting some tats on his fists.

C. B. invites all of us out to Grey Goose Lake for a barbecue on Monday afternoon, but my parents have to work . . . Suckers! He tells my sister to invite as many people as she wants. The 'rents try to communicate to him how big of a mistake that would be, but he says he doesn't care. "I've always dreamed of throwing a party here and having lots of friends around and really doing it up. But I was so poor when I lived here—"

Mom interrupts him. "Will *your* friends be there?"

She asked the question in a very Momma Bear kind of way, so C. B. gets a bit nervous. "Yeah, yeah, Ms. McDougle, and the production team will. We might shoot a party scene, so we need to research it."

She's giving him one of her judgmental looks and adds a sly, "Interesting."

Being a film director might give you a free pass to do whatever you want in most situations, but he's not feeling as good about being the cool adult throwing the high school party anymore. My mom is subtle, but vicious.

11. ASSISTANCE

The weekend flies by, and I'm rudely awoken Monday morning at ten a.m. by the ringing phone. I was up late watching Hilary Idaho movies (for research!). I guess my dad had to go back to work today, thank God. You'd think because I'm a movie star now, he wouldn't expect me to help him with the deck, but you would be wrong. Yesterday I spent four hours at Home Depot picking out wood, instead of thinking about my character! How annoying.

EJ is on the phone and he's pissed. "Yo, your punk ass is really starring in a movie with Hilary Idaho?!"

"Yep."

"And I gotta hear about it from Nicky?"

I apologize for not telling him myself, but it doesn't seem real. I feel more like a laborer than an actor, but hopefully that's about to change. When I wasn't slaving for my dad, I was staring at that script and trying to figure out what the hell I'm going to do with all of these lines. I just feel so unprepared that if I stop focusing for even a second, I'll regret it. So I haven't taken the time to brag about my success. But I'm sure I'll get around to it.

He tells me how hard the CrossFit workout was today and how Bag puked into the water fountain and how it took an hour to get a custodian to mop it out. A bunch of dudes got drinks without knowing how close their faces were to Bag's breakfast. EJ already knows about the party C. B. is throwing at Grey Goose Lake and asks if I want them to pick me up on their way, but I have to decline. He calls me a bitch, so I tell him that I'm meeting up with Hilary Idaho, like it's no big deal, and that I'll try to meet up with them later. He's sooo jealous.

I ride down to the President Hotel for my meeting/fitting. The Kidz Channel has the whole thing rented out. Everyone from the costume department to Sport Coat Phil is staying here. Everyone except C. B., who's renting a house, where, rumor (Jeremy) has it, both Ms. McDougle and Pam have been seen doing the walk of shame on alternate mornings.

I'm thinking that I'm not the only one here to see Hilary, because about twenty paparazzi guys are lurking around the lobby with cameras around their necks and cell phones to their ears. I lock up my bike in the parking garage and check in with a front-desk girl. She tells a massive security guy to "Escort this young man to the penthouse, please."

I wonder if this is Hilary's bodyguard, the one I'm supposed to watch out for. As the elevator doors close, I meet his eyes in the glass reflection. I'm really nervous, so I raise my eyebrows and say, "Penthouse, huh? Dirty, dirty."

He either doesn't know porn or doesn't appreciate porn-related humor. He just glares at me, and I examine my Nikes until the doors open up, right into the suite. Wow, I've never been in a penthouse before. This joint is nice! I try not to look like I'm here to rob the place, as I gaze around the super-swanky apartment. Flowers and baskets of fancy crap are on every available surface. A gaggle of women are walking around the living room area, talking on phones, typing on laptops, and rolling rack after rack of designer clothing into one of the bedrooms.

A three-hundred-pound Victoria Beckham impersonator rushes toward me like my long-lost mother. "Darling! You must be Carter!" She kisses me on the lips and says, "You're adorable, aren't you?!"

After an awkward pause I hesitantly answer, "Yes?"

She laughs like I've told the funniest joke ever, which gets everyone looking at us. I believe this was her intention. The lady is Hilary's mother/manager. She introduces me to her assistant and Hilary's publicist and her assistant, Hilary's wardrobe stylist and her assistant, her trainer, chef, agent, makeup artist, spiritual leader, choreographer, and all of their assistants. I guess it takes a village to raise a star.

Strangely enough, it all seems pretty normal as I talk with each person and her assistant. I'm thinking that in order to become a "somebody" you've got to have a "nobody" working for you. How great would I be if I had a flunky keeping me on track, reminding me to do my homework and put on deodorant in the morning? I'm gawking at the room, spacing off, when I feel someone watching me. The bedroom door is open, and I see a large eyeball peeking through the slit between the door and the wall, just above the middle hinge. If I had a personal assistant, I would ask him if he thinks that's Hilary Idaho's eyeball. If her belly button were showing through the crack, I'd know for sure. We stare at each other for a beat before the eye disappears.

The wardrobe stylist's assistant tells me they are ready to start the fitting and asks if I'd like anything to drink, but tells me all they have is Diet Coke.

"Oh, I'll just take some water, then."

She replies, "*All* we have is Diet Coke."

I tell her, "I'm good," and explain that my sister is going to be her new assistant.

She makes a face and sighs, "Yeah, I've been informed."

"I think you two will get along."

I start trying on a bunch of old Levi's and T-shirts. They refer to them as "vintage." It's pretty much the exact thing I wear every day and have a closet full of, but when I suggest that I could bring some of my own stuff, they completely ignore me. They seem totally stressed like this is the hardest job ever. I must be missing something about it. They rip the clothes off the hangers as if someone's life was on the line. I ask where I should change, and the stylist looks at her assistant for a translation. I could swear she spoke English a second ago. The assistant yells, "We don't have time for this! You change right here."

"In front of you guys?"

The stylist barks, "Yes!" without a hint of an accent.

I mutter, "Okay" as I drop my drawers. I'm putting on the first pair of jeans when the assistant squats down and points at my package. She asks, "Would his character wear whitey tighties?"

The stylist glares at my BVDs for an answer. She shakes her head and screams, "I have no idea! It's not in my notes! Get C. B. on the phone! We have to figure this out!"

I stand around and they snap photos of me in my underwear. It's pretty freaky until the stylist gets a text and yells, "Whitey tighties are a go! Get me three different kinds in three different sizes!"

Thank God my sister is coming tomorrow to lessen

their workload. I try on the jeans, and they snap more pho-tos. At one point, the assistant thought I was moving too slow, so she reaches around my waist and unbuttons the top button before unzipping the fly. She's about to pull the jeans down when I grab the waistband and yell, "Wait!"

I'm not used to women removing my pants yet. Maybe someday I'll be able to handle it, but today is not that day. I'm a bit too "excited" to be seen in my undies for a while. I ask to use the restroom, and they sigh with frustration.

I try on a hundred T-shirts and jeans before they tell me we're done. They're running around trying to find the per-fect shoes for my character. I've tried about ten pair when the assistant notices my old Nikes on the ground. She squeals with delight, "Oh my God, who pulled these?!"

The costume designer looks at my stinky-ass running shoes like they were sent from heaven, and orders me to try them on with the rest of my costume.

I try to explain, "They're my shoes."

But she thinks I'm some kind of Method actor who only speaks for his character. She replies, "YES! They're perfect, aren't they? We've done it again, girls!"

The assistant adds, "It's like they're molded to his feet!" as she's putting them into a plastic bag.

I decide not to waste my breath with more explanations, so I ask, "Can I borrow those shoes . . . to help me get into character?"

The costume designer seems nervous about allowing the precious grass-stained sneakers out of her sight, but eventu-ally says, "Yeah, C. B. told me you were a serious actor. . . . Be careful with them."

I tell her I'll try, and they furiously get to work, tailoring the clothes they've chosen. I'm putting my Levi's back on—the ones that already fit—when I notice Hilary Idaho sitting by the window reading the book version of *Down Gets Out*. My boys would crap themselves, and I'm surprised that I haven't. The light is hitting her just right, and she's kind of glowing. She's scary skinny but very pretty. She's rocking a short Japanese robe. Her manicured feet are propped up in the window, so I can see most of her long tan legs. She's smiling as she reads.

I slip on my (vintage) T-shirt before walking over. I'm not as nervous as I should be, because I've got the perfect question: "Where are you at in the story?"

She looks up at me and smiles. "Ohhh, it's my second time through; they're at that point where things are starting to go well for Chris, and they're falling in love and pretending to be lord and lady of the manor."

I know exactly the part she's referring to, so I put on a goofy British accent and say, "Madame, did you pay the light bill?"

She giggles and does a similar accent, but hers sounds totally authentic when she bellows, "We really must get a new cleaning lady!"

We both laugh, and I say, "You obviously like the book."

She softly corrects me. "I love it; it's the best book I've ever read."

"Me, too!" I say, offering up a high five, which she slaps like a pro. "I have to confess, I haven't read a ton of books, though."

She whisper/laughs, "I haven't either. I don't attend the most challenging school."

I should be freaking out about how well this is going and how nice she's being to me and how much of her upper thigh is visible, but I'm not because I'm a trained player/journalist/warrior, and I fire out another question. "Where do you go to school?"

She motions around the room and says, "You're looking at it; I've never been to a real school. I've always just had set teachers and tutors."

"Must be nice?" That's more of a statement, but I try to say it like a question.

She shrugs. "I don't know if it is or it isn't, but it's all I know. I usually have trouble talking to regular kids."

"Me, too! I'm Carter, by the way."

We shake hands, and she replies, "I know, I've heard all about you."

"You have? Cool . . . So, what's your name?"

She releases my hand and looks confused, so I say, "I'm kidding, I know who you are, Hilary." She looks really embarrassed to have missed the joke, so I sit down next to her and explain, "Sorry. Sarcasm is taught heavily in *my* school."

"Well, you'll have to catch me up. I'm pretty hopeless when it comes to humor."

"You do a great British accent."

As if she's Mary Poppins herself, she says, "Yes I do! Don't I?"

"See? That's funny."

"Is it?"

"Yeah, trust me, I'm a regular kid," I say, and bust a perfect wink!

The wink may have been too much, because she looks away and the conversation dies. So I bust out another question. "Did you learn that accent for the Princess Journal movies?"

She replies, "Yeah, I got pretty good by the third one."

"Oh, I've only seen two of them. My sister has, I mean . . . so I've only watched bits and pieces of them."

She laughs. "Carter, you can tell me you've seen the Princess Journals . . . I was in them . . . I won't judge."

I confess, "Yeah, I've seen them both, like, five times."

She pushes me and says, "Gay-wad."

She starts laughing hysterically, and I say, "Dude, you don't need any help. You're a total smart-ass!"

She giggles. "I'm not usually."

"Unless you really think I'm gay . . . then that would make you a total bitch for saying that."

She laughs for about five more minutes and then tells me that the third Princess Journal movie never actually came out. When I ask her what happened, she kind of dodges the question and explains how movies get made all the time and never get distributed. "They run out of money, or they don't test well."

I think "test" loosely translates to "it sucks."

She explains that it wasn't even released on DVD because it was worth more to the producers as a tax write-off than as a flop.

I quietly ask, "How did C. B.'s first movie, *Genoa Eyes*, get distribution?"

She tells me that it didn't until it won the Cannes Film Festival, and art films don't have to make as much money as regular movies. She obviously loved *Genoa Eyes*, like Abby did, so I don't bag on it.

She sighs, "C. B. is such a brilliant director. I hope I don't let him down."

I nod and say, "Me, too."

She laughs. "You don't have anything to worry about. C. B. loves you, Carter. I've only had one meeting with him, and all he talked about was you. He really thinks you're special. A lot of my guy friends wanted this part."

I add, "I'm probably a lot cheaper."

"That's why Phil likes you, but C. B. believes you have 'raw talent.' He wants me to hang out with you as much as I can, so I can learn from you."

I gasp, "Learn from me? You've done a hundred movies!"

"He wants me to forget everything I know about acting, and just 'be normal,' but I'm not sure what that means. You know, I shot my first commercial when I was two months old? I've sold ten million records, been in thirty-seven national commercials, and I've actually only done twelve movies, but ninety-eight episodes of *The Get Up Gang*."

"What are you, thirty-five years old?"

"Sixteen."

"I guess I can try to help you be normal, but you've got to help me with the movie stuff."

"It's a deal," she says.

We high-five like longtime friends. I know that I should ask her another question, but I'm feeling like such a badass because someone has finally noticed my "raw talent" that I try for a joke. "Okay, Hilary, first thing we've got to do is get rid of this kimono."

She squints her eyes and asks, "Naked? That's how I become a regular girl?"

"Dude, are you sassin' me on the first day of training?"

She comes in close and whispers, "Be careful what you ask an actress to do, because we're usually up for anything."

"And I will stop you right there, because it seems like you're flirting with me. And normal girls do *not* flirt with me."

She nods. "Got it. No flirting. Should I write this down, Mr. Carter?"

"See, it still seems like you're flirting."

"Sorry, I do that."

I clarify. "No, don't misunderstand. You're allowed to flirt with guys. I see girls around here doing it all the time. I'm just letting you know that they do not do it with me."

She gives me a sly smile and says, "I will try to restrain myself."

"Thank you."

She says, "No-no, thank you."

I smile because I'm officially flirting my ass off with Hilary Idaho. This is championship flirting, and I'm involved! I'm so cool, but how? I can't stop to figure out what I'm doing or not doing. *Keep it loose and use your instincts, playa!* I want to keep doing this for the rest of my life. *Hit her with a question!*

"Are you really dating Zac-Michael Wienus?"

She laughs. "No, we broke up. Don't you read the tabloids?"

I shake my head, and she seems very happy that I don't. She adds, "Well, I just read that I'm engaged to a Saudi prince, so that's a new development."

I nod and say, "Cool, so there's still hope for that lost Princess Journal movie."

She stops laughing and asks, "Do you have any questions for me, Carter? About filmmaking?"

A million of them fly through my head, but the one I grab on to is: "Okay, you and I are supposed to make out at the end of the movie, right? Do we need to rehearse that, or do we just wing it?"

She thinks for a second before she says, "Now who's flirting?"

My mouth drops. "Oh, wow, I was, wasn't I? I didn't even mean to."

She giggles. "Sure you didn't. You're a player, aren't you?"

I shake my head like I don't know what she's talking about . . . but I do! My killer instincts are out and in full effect. I shrug like a pimp and say, "Must be that 'raw talent.'"

She giggles, but stiffens up when a large softball coach of a woman stomps over to us from the costume racks. The woman's voice is way deeper than mine. She murmurs, "Ms. Idaho, your Pilates lesson starts in four minutes. It's time for Mr. Carter to go."

Hilary stands up and screeches in the lady's face, "MATILDA, how dare you! The director of this project has asked me to spend as much time with this boy as I can. For you to interrupt our meeting is totally unprofessional and unacceptable. Now go!" She stomps her foot and points to the bedroom, but Matilda just stands there and looks down at me with contempt.

I'm thinking that this is the bodyguard I was supposed to watch out for, but I may need to watch out for Hilary. That was a mood swing even my sister would bow down to.

Matilda calmly says, "We need to stick to the schedule. Perhaps he would like to do some Pilates with you so that he can experience some of your world before you rush off to embrace his."

It seemed like she was listening to our conversation. And just so you know, if someone asks you if you want to do some Pilates, tell them NO! It's worse than CrossFit, but in a totally different way. The costume ladies give me some shorts, and we go down to the hotel's gym with this hot-ass trainer lady in black spandex. The gym doesn't have any weights or fans or rock music playing. It's just a few wooden medieval torture devices called "reformers" with pulleys, straps, springs, and harnesses that you lash yourself to and try to grunt and rip your body into these impossible positions. It's all about your "core" and your pain threshold.

Hilary is going about this program as if she were born doing it. She ties her skinny body into a pretzel and then unties it over and over again with fluid motion and small changes. It's beautiful to watch, but after a few minutes, I understand the machine's name and I'm completely "reformed." I'll do whatever it asks. My hips are dislocated and my left leg is wrapped around my head. I'm looking directly at my own ass and supporting all of my body weight with two fingers. Every muscle in my body is trembling with pain, but I don't dare release the pose for fear that this contraption will shoot me across the room! After an hour of this hell, the lady tells me that I'm through and I've done a great job. I know she's lying, but I feel three inches taller and I'm as upright as an action figure. If my chest wasn't twitching and flexing every few minutes, I might want to try this workout again . . . after a few weeks rest.

12. HOW WE ROLL

Next, Hilary and I take a shower together. . . . Not really, but in my head we do. I use a guest bathroom in the suite, and my shower takes longer than it should. Mostly I was trying to figure out the best way to help her get into character as a normal Merrian teenager. She can't go to the mall because she'll get mobbed. The pool is out because of her spray tan, and I can't take her to the Merrian High weight room until my chest stops twitching. I decide to take her out to Grey Goose Lake for C. B.'s party.

I borrow a T-shirt and some board shorts from the costume department while the whole circus prepares Hilary for the change of venue. The makeup ladies descend on her like a NASCAR pit crew. Hot rollers, hair spray, airbrushes, nail files, and polish applicators all working at the same time. I don't get to watch the bikini waxing, but I can imagine how it went down, and it was beautiful. I have to use the restroom (because I drank a lot of water during the Pilates session). I come out of the bathroom ten minutes later (I drank a lot), and Hilary is finally ready. Her little outfit probably cost more than my bike, but all I can see is the strings of her bikini poking out of the tops of her shorts and tank top. *Please, God, let me see Hilary Idaho in a bikini!*

About ten of us make our way down to the parking lot. I realize why everyone was wearing sunglasses in the elevator, when the doors pop open and a gang of paparazzi start yelling, clicking, and flashing away. I can't see a damn thing so Hilary grabs my hand and leads me through the chaos. We jump in the back of an Escalade, and I try to get my eyes to work again.

Three matching black SUVs roll out of the garage in tight formation with ours in the middle. I try to give a tour of Merrian, but it's hard to tell the driver where to go because he has to radio the lead Escalade to makes the turns ahead of us. I'm used to riding my bike or being driven by someone, so I keep forgetting to give them enough notice to coordinate.

I ask, "Can't we just take the lead?"

Matilda sternly replies, "Leave the security to us, Mr. Carter."

It's also hard to talk over all of the ladies on their cell phones, and her mom keeps interrupting me to say, "Oh, isn't that quaint?!"

I cancel the tour and just tell them to go out to the lake. As we're rolling along, a motorcycle keeps zooming up to our windows. There's a guy riding on the back, taking pictures of us through the tinted glass. Matilda points at him and fires an imaginary finger gun at him as he passes. I laughed the first time she did it, but after the third, I realize that she's actually practicing. She catches me watching her and points the imaginary weapon at me. "What happened to your face?" she asks, like I've done something wrong.

"Bike jump went bad."

Hilary asks, "Are you in the X Games?"

I chuckle and am about to say "Yeah, right," when I cut myself off and just say, "Yeah."

The makeup ladies nod as if they're impressed. Matilda just flexes her jaw like she knows I'm lying. She must be ex-CIA or something.

Hilary starts telling a story about how she used to date the skater Ryan Sheckler and what a dork he is, when I hear a call come into the driver's earpiece: "We have a situation coming up on the right."

I look ahead of the lead SUV and see my boys pedaling along in a big pack, screwing up traffic on the two-lane road. Hormone's dad must have confiscated the CRX, because he's riding his old GT again. J-Low is in front, and Nutt is riding in the drainage ditch. Bitchy Nicky is a passenger on EJ's pegs, and she doesn't look happy about it. Doc is riding on Bag's pegs, and he seems okay with it. I ask the driver to pull up along side of them; Matilda nods that it's okay. All of the cyclists stiffen as our big-ass truck slows down to match their speed. I roll the window down and their tense faces all explode with relief when I pop out and say, "S'up, bitches!"

Nutt rides out of the ditch and grabs the window frame as we roll along. "What the hell are you doin', Carter?"

"I'm just chillin' with my new friend, Hilary Idaho, here." She sticks her head out the window and smiles at them. Their jaws drop at the same time.

Bag is only able to say, "Son of a . . ." before he drives off the road and crashes into the drainage ditch, sending Doc flying headfirst into the embankment.

The ladies in the car are obviously not used to seeing guys smash themselves into various states of brain damage, like I am. They scream, "Oh NOOOO" and "That poor boy!"

Doc just lies there for a second, but I assure them, "He's fine."

The driver has slowed down to a crawl but asks Matilda, "Should I stop?"

Hilary answers, "Yes, you asshole!" so he does. She and I hop out of the car and jog toward the stalled caravan of BMXs. Matilda follows us closely. By the time we get to them, Doc is holding his shoulder, and Nutt is waving his hand at him and demanding, "How many fingers?!"

I give a few high fives and introduce everyone to Hilary. It's kind of weird because my boys and Nicky are all staring at Hilary's boobs to see if they're real or not, and a photographer is running around us, clicking and flashing away.

I try to cough orders to my friends by covering my mouth and barking, "Whrr-raise the gaze!" That's something our football coach came up with. If you see one of your boys staring at a chick's breasts and he's not aware of it, you're supposed to pretend to cough the commands until they realize and finally "raise the gaze," but there's just too much going on around here.

Hilary finally crosses her arms and asks me, "Did you ride your bicycle to the hotel, Carter?" I nod that I did, and she motions to EJ and his hose beast. "I thought you were going to help me become a regular kid. I'm trying to get into character here. If this is how you guys get around, then that's how I want to do it."

Nicky jumps in. "Hilary, this is not how I travel!"

Everyone ignores her, and I shrug. "Okay. E, could we please borrow your bike? We're going to the lake, so you guys can just ride in one of these SUVs."

I was only offering a ride to EJ and Nicky, but I'm pretty relieved when everyone else piles their bikes into the front vehicle and jumps into the back two. The makeup ladies do not seem impressed by these sweaty boys climbing over and smashing into them. Matilda is the last one into the Escalade and shows me her finger gun, threateningly, before shutting the door. Hilary and I are left alone on the road . . . with this damn camera guy clicking away. Shouldn't Matilda be intimidating him instead of me?

"Ever ridden on axle pegs?" I ask Hilary.

She smiles and says, "Zac-Michael has a Ducati; I've been on the back of that."

I look down at EJ's ratty old BMX that he leaves out in the rain, and say, "Pretty much the same thing. We may go a bit slower, for safety, but there's no better way to take in the sights, and it's a hell of a calf workout."

She climbs on and grabs my shoulders as we get rolling. I'm pretty nervous that I'll crash her into the ditch, but she's ridiculously light. I wouldn't even notice her back there if she wasn't giggling and yelling, "This is so much fun!"

Zac-Michael and his Ducati can suck it!

I try to think of questions, but the only thing I can come up with is about me, so it probably doesn't count. "Do you think I look like one of the Wienus Bros?"

"God, NOOO!"

"Jeez, no need to be rude—"

She replies, "You're way cuter and about a foot taller."

"I'm taller than the tallest Wienus?"

"Yeah, he's about five foot three."

The parade of Escalades is rolling along with us at a

blazing three miles an hour and trying to choke me out with exhaust. I wish the photographer would stop zipping by us. The windows of the SUVs are tinted, but I can still see my boys flipping me off in there. I'm pretty busy with the pedaling, but I find the focus to fire questions back to Hilary and answer her when she asks what I know about Ms. McDougle and the Saur mansion. She seems pretty interested in Merrian and my friends and how we live. I tell her that she seems like one of those Nat-Geo chicks who goes into the jungle to study the monkeys. I try to explain what I know about my world . . . which isn't much, as it turns out. I've never really thought about the reasons we talk the way we do or act how we do or why my dad wants to build his own deck as opposed to hiring a construction crew. I have no idea. I'm even more worthless when it comes to the female questions. "Girls around here are really a mystery to me, but you should talk to Abby. I think she's going to be your stand-in."

She replies, "Cool. Is she your girlfriend?"

I tell her that she *was*, and Hilary squeezes my shoulders before saying, "Her loss."

I forget how to ride the bike for a second, but then I'm back. She even wants to know where I get my underwear, and I have to tell her, "I have no idea. New ones just show up in my drawer every once in a while."

After about twenty minutes, I'm sick of the inquisition and feeling the Pilates workout in my legs. I'm happy to be rolling up to the Grey Goose security shack and not having to sneak in through the golf course, like usual. The lead driver talks to the old guard in the booth and he waves us all through, but stops the paparazzi motorcycle. I follow the lead Escalade past the awesome clubhouse and the diving boards and swimming beach. Everyone is staring at us as we roll by. I'd like to keep going to the rope swing, but about halfway around the lake I see a gang of crappy cars and C. B.'s Ferrari in the driveway of a super-modern house and hear music blasting. I see that my parents have lent my sister the Accord, because it's parked beside the lake (the bumper is actually underwater). The entire roof of C. B.'s house is a deck that overlooks the water, and it's filled with high school kids. The SUVs slow to a stop and the doors open. I hit the brakes and Hilary steps off of the pegs, laughing. "You weren't kidding about the calf workout."

"Pretty fun, yeah?"

She smiles and says, "Absolutely."

I look up to the roof deck and see two hundred eyes peering down at us. A guy's voice yells, "Carter's a tool!" and then a girl pukes over the railing, almost hitting the Ferrari.

Reluctantly, I lean the bike against a retaining wall and sigh, "So, this is a high school party."

She grabs my hand and says, "Let's do it."

You can tell Matilda and her mom don't want her to go inside. But it's for her work, so they allow her a few feet of freedom, for research sake, and hope that the monkeys don't throw too much crap at her.

EJ and Nicky walk in ahead of us, but everyone is gawking at Hilary. She squeezes my hand like a little kid who's just entered a scary place, but the house is beautiful. She whispers in my ear, "This place is straight out of *Dwell* magazine."

I nod like I've got a subscription to this magazine I've never heard of. There are big awesome paintings everywhere and sculptures on stands. It makes me nervous to think about my past experience with high school parties and whole houses getting torn apart by drunk dickheads, but the walls are intact, so far. I'm staring at a statue of a man's head with a hole drilled through it, and trying to figure out what it means, when I catch my sister looking at me. She points to Hilary and angrily mouths the word, "Focus!"

There's a staff of people cleaning up after everyone, and we're told that there's a bar and a chef working on the rooftop grill. All of the kids are staring at us as we ascend the stairs. I can see the redness in Hilary's cheeks and feel how uncomfortable she is. I try to think of good questions, but all I come up with is, "Is this like an L.A. party?"

Sadly, she says, "Yeah."

We're headed toward the railing to check out the awesome view of Grey Goose Lake when I feel Abby's tractor beam being fired at me. I turn and lock eyes with her. Seeing me standing here, holding hands with the girl who got her part in the movie, seems too much for her to deal with. Tears fill her eyes, and she retreats down the stairs.

I try to let go of Hilary's hand, and say, "I'll be right back."

But she won't release my digits, and demands, "No! You can't leave me, Carter."

I see Abby's ponytail disappear into the house, and I give Hilary a forced wink.

C. B. weaves his way over from the bar and greets us with hugs. "Good, you two are getting along?"

Hilary seems to relax for a second and tells him how much fun she had riding out here, and I tell him about Pilates being worse than CrossFit. He stops a waiter and asks what we'd like to drink. Since Hilary is studying me, she waits to see what I'll order, and I know it would seem cool to ask for a beer, because everyone else is boozing, but I'm dying of thirst, so I ask, "Do you guys have any Gatorade?"

C. B. smiles, and Hilary asks for a Diet Coke. The waiter goes to hook us up, and C. B. wants to know if I've seen Ms. McDougle. He seems disappointed that I haven't, but he better hope she doesn't show up and find all of these high school kids drinking at his house, because she'll bust his ass. But I don't want to sound like an after-school special, so I keep it to myself. A few girls have asked Hilary for her auto-graph, and she poses for a bunch of cell-phone snapshots. The party keeps getting bigger and bigger, and everyone is just watching her . . . except her mom, who's settling in with her third martini. The makeup ladies are doing shots with Nick Brock and Lynn. I've only known Hilary for a few hours, but I really like her, and I know that she's a superstar, but I kind of feel sorry for her. She keeps squeezing my hand tighter and tighter. When I look down at her kung-fu grip, she tries to play off her discomfort with a fake smile. I know that she just wants to blend in here and study everyone else for her character, but it seems kind of impossible, so I ask her, "Hey, do you wanna do somethin' cool?"

She nods, and we slowly work our way back down the stairs. "Do we have to tell your entourage where we're going?" I ask.

She gives me an ornery look and says, "Let's not."

I glance around, but don't see Abby anywhere, and can almost feel Matilda's finger gun pointing at the back of my head as we cut through the kitchen and duck out a side door. We run around the house and surprise Nutt, who's peeing onto a fancy bush. I give him a push that sends his legs into the urinated branches.

He cries, "Damn it, Carter!"

I yell back to him, "Sorry, dog, I'm trying to show Hilary how we roll!"

None of the Escalade drivers are paying attention, so I grab EJ's bike, and she jumps on the pegs like she's been doing it for years. As we roll out, her mom yells down from the roof deck, "HILARY, where the hell are you going?"

I squeeze the brakes, but Hilary orders me to keep pedaling, before yelling back, "We're just going to go do something cool!"

Her mom exclaims, "WHAT?!" as I weave through the bottleneck of illegally parked cars. Matilda rushes out the front door as the lead SUV fires to life. She jumps in the passenger seat, and I hear the horn blast as the driver finds his fat-ass Escalade unable to follow my sleek BMX.

Hilary is squealing with delight and jerking my shoulders all around.

I yell, "Don't make me wreck. I'm in enough trouble as it is!"

We zip around the lake and cut across a footbridge that leads to the golf course before I dip off the cart path and narrowly miss getting whacked by an old lady about to tee off. We angle onto the wooded trail that leads to the rope swing. We hop off the bike, and she follows me down to the water's edge.

I doubt she'll think this is as cool as I do, but I strip off my shirt and pick up the old knotted rope. I trek backward up the small incline, jump as high as I can (not that high), and swing out over the lake. I wait till the last minute before I release, spin around, smile at her and yell, "WHOOOAHH!!!" before I splash into the cool lake and yell, "YEEESSSS!!!" under the water. I come up for air and find Hilary giggling on the bank.

"You wanna try?" I ask as I climb out. She strips down to her bikini (thank you!) and takes the rope from me. She's smiling from ear to ear as she steps back a few feet. You can see her rib bones as she leaps into the air and glides out over the water with a gleeful scream. For just a second I feel like such a pimp for bringing her here and showing her something so cool and out of the ordinary . . . but that second passes. The rope reaches its climax and she does *not* let go. I guess I wasn't specific enough with the instructions. I saw this happen to a younger kid last year, and it was not pretty. The rope is headed back to the tree whether you're attached or not. And bark is not as soft as it looks. Her glee turns to terror as she sees the thick trunk getting closer and closer.

"Release!" I order, but she's got that Pilates-kung-fu grip in her fingers and a deer-in-headlights look in her eyes.

Just before she smashes into the tree, my feet leave the ground. I bury my shoulder in her tiny waist and blast her away from the tree. My football coach would have been proud of the form tackle, but horrified at who I delivered it to. Hilary yells out a painful, "Ouhhhh!" and lets go of the rope so we can crash into the muddy bank. I'm lying on top of her as she's convulsing in the slop.

At this point my debate is, Would it be faster to carry her back to C. B.'s house, or leave her here while I ride over there and call the ambulance?

But I'm super relieved to find that she's actually laughing.

"Oh my God, I'm such an idiot!" she cackles. Her face and hair are all muddy, and she's rolling around.

I sit up and chuckle. "No, it happens to the best of us. Are you okay?"

I stop laughing (and breathing) when she sits up. Her swimming suit has come . . . ajar. It's twisted around and both triangles have moved three inches to the left. . . . Neither one is doing its job anymore.

She's oblivious to the peep show as she giggles. "My mother would have killed me!"

"Uh . . . uuum . . ." I say, motioning to her chest.

"This mud is probably good for your skin," she adds, smearing it onto her cheeks.

I hear a rustling in the woods, but don't look away from her chest as I mutter, "Hey, um, your, your boobs are out."

"What?" she asks, and then looks down before busting out laughing again.

I try to make her feel less embarrassed. "I h-h-hate it when that happens!"

I close my eyes and try to take a mental picture of what I just witnessed so I can reflect on it later and brag to my boys with great detail.

When I open them, I expect to see her bikini restored to its original position, but it's not. It is now on the ground next to me, and a ninety-six-percent naked Hilary Idaho dives into the lake!

No need for the mental pictures, because my boys will *never* believe this. She swims around, and I hear that same rustling in the bushes. I'm waiting for Ashton Kutcher to bust through the leaves and tell me I'm being "Punked!" or some kid is coming down to use the rope swing and is about to get the shock of his life! She dips her hair back into the lake and steps out onto the bank. A clicking, cracking sound is coming from somewhere, and I just know someone is coming, so I extend my hands to cover her exposed breasts.

"Sorry, sorry, uh, G-G-Grey Goose isn't that kind of lake, I don't think."

She doesn't freak out about my hand placement, but simply explains, "Carter, I swim like this all the time in France. No tanlines."

"Well, that does make sense, but uh, w-w-we're a long ways from France and I think people are coming."

She just laughs. "My breasts are all over the Internet anyway. . . ."

"They are? I haven't seen 'em." (Liar.)

"You're seeing them now."

"No, I'm not! I'm blocking them, see? And I-I-I'm not like an expert or anything; I've only felt one boob . . . a pair, I mean . . . One girl's breasts is all that I can draw on for my research, but yours feel pretty real."

Annoyed, she responds, "That's because they are."

"Oh, I just heard . . ."

"Yeah, I know what you heard, but it's not true, like most of the crap they print." She seems annoyed that I've brought her back into the world she's trying to escape. "I thought you didn't read the tabloids."

"I don't. I just heard that. Does anyone actually *read* them?"

She places her hands over mine (because I'm still cupping Hilary Idaho's boobies!) and asks, "Would you prefer it if I put my top back on?"

I cannot believe what I'm saying when I sigh, "Yes."

Once her breasts have been reluctantly released and put away, we start having a good time again. She tries the rope swing another time and doesn't fly quite as high, but she does let go at the right time and enjoys it a lot more. Who wouldn't? When she comes to the surface, she squeals, "Oh my God!!! That's like the best drug ever!"

I say, "Hells yeah it is!" but I don't think she's talking about Advil. I try to show off with a flip, but bust a *SMACK*, instead.

She laughs at my pain and goes again. She screams, "It's like flying!" in midair.

I'm a lot stronger this summer from working out, but I can only do about ten swings before my grip is shot. Hilary is wicked buff from doing Pilates since birth, so she's unstoppable. She starts doing gainers in no time. I give her a boost so she can reach higher on the rope, and my hand is totally touching Hilary Idaho's butt! For some reason, it's not really that hot. It's not like I'm grabbing a dude's butt, but I'm not that attracted to her. Probably because there's no chance of her being into me, or I'm turned off by her ribs sticking out. We're having fun, though, so I try not to worry about it. We swing off of it together a few times and swim around for a bit before I climb out to take a break. She's floating out in the water, staring up at the sky (her boobs are real . . . and buoyant).

She softly says, "I like it here."

I reply, "That's because you've got a great tour guide."

I'm not sure if she heard me, because she asks if I've ever been to Hawaii.

I just laugh. "The only flying I've ever done is here."

She raises her head and looks at me, so I clarify. "I've never been on an airplane."

She makes a face of pity and says, "Well, I went last year with some friends, to party. It was me and the Wienus Bros, the Molsen Twins, Tito, and a bunch of other kids. We were staying at this private villa and we had champagne and lobster out on this big terrace overlooking a perfect blue lagoon. There were these local boys, a bit younger than us, swinging out into the water on this old rope, and they seemed to be having so much fun. I wanted to go over and hang out with them, because there we were, celebrities, paying all this money to have the best drugs and food, but we weren't having half as good a time as these kids who'd just tied a rope to a branch and were splashing around in the water together. Zac-Michael called security, and they shooed them away and cut down the rope. It made me so sad when he did that. He couldn't stand to see 'nobodies' enjoying themselves, and that's disgusting. I had other stuff going on. My dad had just left for New York and he didn't tell us when he was coming back, so that may have caused it. The third Princess Journal was going down in flames about that time, but it was the look on those boys' faces that pushed me over the edge. They were like, 'Who do you think you are?' and I couldn't deal. I got so wasted that day, and I stayed wasted. We got kicked out of the villa after I trashed it, and my mom had to fly out and get me. She checked me into rehab when I got home, and I got Matilda as a Christmas present."

I'm just sitting on the bank, looking at her. She's telling a story about how sad her life is, but she really seems to be enjoying herself here. She's in no hurry to get back to her suite at the President Hotel or her movie star life. I know that I've never been to Hawaii, and she may pity me because of it, but I feel so bad for her.

"What do you do at rehab?" I ask.

"Arts and crafts," she says with a laugh.

I smile at her little joke, but I don't say anything so she can answer the question. She shrugs. "It's in the desert so there's nothing to do except talk about our problems. You know, why we use, and why it sucks to be a celebrity. We work on ways to stay clean."

I probably shouldn't, but I try for a joke. "I use Lever 2000, so I'm clean and also moisturized."

She doesn't seem to know that brand of soap, so I try a different style of humor. "Does *The Get Up Gang* get a group discount at rehab?"

She kind of laughs (thank you) and says, "We should."

"Yeah, you guys are a mess."

She tries to explain. "Every one of us has been working since we were little, supporting our families. You know, my dad is a theater actor, and he's great at it, but he doesn't make enough money to live in New York. My mom is my manager. I'm making all this money that I know I'll never see. I live in a fishbowl. If this movie flops, it'll probably be your fault because you don't have enough box office pull to sell tickets, but I'll get blamed. I won't get any more serious acting work. You only get a few chances before you're stuck on the reality TV circuit and VH1 produces *What Happened to Hilary?* My last album sucked. I eat 1200 calories a day. No more, no less. I take voice, dance, diction, and movement lessons every day. And I can't complain about any of it because it's supposed to be fun. But it's not, when you have to do it. Everyone thinks my life is so great, and I'm a bitch for not appreciating it. So I used to drink or take pills or whatever because people offered them to me, and they made me forget about all of it for a little while. I think that's why the others do it, too. I've been clean for two months, and I feel good, but I've been on lockdown and haven't been working. And working is the hardest part for me. If I really was a regular kid and this was my life and I went to a real school, I know I could stay clean."

I toss a pebble into the water and ask, "Acting in a movie is going to be harder than I think, isn't it?"

She replies, "No, I just make it hard. I feel like, when those cameras roll, I have to be perfect. I need to look perfect and feel perfect, and if I have to take a shortcut to get there, then so be it. I'm a professional and that means doing whatever it takes. Zac-Michael is the opposite. He has to be employed at all times, or he turns into a junkie. Phil Coates knows that, too, and he still didn't hire him."

I'd like to avoid the subject of why Zac-Michael didn't get the part in *Down Gets Out*, so I ask, "Does Phil know that working is hard for you?"

She nods, so I ask, "Do your parents know?"

She doesn't answer that one, so I inquire, "Do you know who Dickens is?"

She lifts her head and looks over at me like she doesn't, so I explain, "He's this old-time writer who told stories about kids working in factories, and sometimes they'd get crushed by a machine or get their little hands caught in the gears or something horrible like that. . . . I think your life might be considered, in a Hollywood sort of way, *very Dickens*."

112

She smiles and puts her head back into the water. She softly sighs, "Do you know, I didn't even go swimming in Hawaii?"

I break the somber mood by quietly grabbing the rope and swinging out over her. I yell, "You're swimmin' with the locals now!" and bust a cannonball right next to her, *BOOOM!!!* We get into a playful splash fight, but stop when we hear a crashing sound in the bushes.

Matilda busts through like a linebacker on safari. "Goddamn it, Hilary, you know the rules! You're never to leave my side. What the hell have you two been doing?"

I know we haven't done anything wrong, but I feel sooo guilty. Hilary swims to the bank and climbs out screeching, "Nothing, we're just talking!"

Matilda sarcastically pants, "Yeah right . . . This'll go on my report, and you're submitting a urine sample!"

I interrupt, "W-w-we've just been swimming."

She looks down at me with daggers coming out of her eyeballs when she sneers, "Nobody asked you a question! You're in big trouble, young man."

What the hell? I don't think she can get me fired from the movie, but I'm terrified of her tracking skills. Hilary angrily puts on her shirt and stomps up the path to the waiting Escalades. Matilda growls at me as I slip my shoes on and grab the bike.

As I get to the road, the three SUVs speed away and leave me in the dust. I wave to them and say, "No, I'm good! I don't need a ride . . . because I've got this bike here, and I'm really into the environment . . . and your trucks aren't responsible enough for me." The paparazzi motorcycle blows past. The guy on back is smiling. He's covered in leaves and clutches his cameras in one hand while giving me a thumbs-up with the other.

I start to ride back to C. B.'s but am almost killed by my parents' Accord barreling around a curve, followed by twenty other cars running from the police cruisers that are now parked in front of the *Dwell* house. Ms. McDougle's Corrolla is sitting next to the Ferrari, and I think I know who called the cops. I don't stop to find out what's going on, because I hear a golfer yelling in the distance and turn around to see my boys riding across the ninth hole. I take off to catch up with them and ask how they got their bikes out of the Escalades, who got busted by the cops, and maybe talk about whose boobs we've touched this afternoon.

13. IN CHARACTER

Sport Coat Phil calls the next day to bitch me out for taking Hilary off the reservation. "You're on thin ice, Carter. I wanted to fire you, but Hilary and C. B. threw a fit, so you've got one more chance. But if you screw up, even a little bit, or if you compromise Ms. Idaho's safety or jeopardize her career, you'll never work again."

I know he means that he'll try to keep me from acting in any more movies. But I give him the smart-ass treatment. "Not even, like, a lifeguarding job?" (C. B. is always a dick to Phil; I think it's rubbing off on me.) I'm hoping he'll think that his threats don't bother me, but they do. I really want to be in this movie, and I want to be great, so I apologize for being a prick and assure him that I won't screw up.

Phil explains the shooting schedule, and I furiously write down everything he says on my arm and hand. But just before he hangs up, he tells me, "This could all change in a moment's notice, so you should be prepared for anything, just in case."

Dang it, I just made a mess of myself for nothing. I've come to realize that if someone tells you something and then follows it with, "This may change," they're pretty sure that's what's going to happen.

I'm not allowed to hang out with Hilary for a few days,

so I hit the library and check out a bunch of books on acting, as well as Daniel Day-Lewis's and Marlon Brando's biographies. My boys call to go to the gym and to the pool, but I decline their invitations and keep reading. Stanislavsky and Uta Hagen may be great teachers, but they're terrible writers. McDougle says that these are the principles she uses to teach all of her classes, but they don't make much sense to me. I thought it would be a step-by-step "how to" guide to becoming another person, but these books get all lost in "psychophysical" and "psychological realism," and they use all of these big words. The books even stink a bit like poop, as if the writers were just pulling this information straight out of their asses. I know exactly why these books were never turned into movies, and I decide that this crap is for theater actors. And since I'm trying to be a film actor now, I take them back to the library and start in on the two biographies.

They're so good, and so much more helpful. It's fun to see how these great actors grew up and what makes them tick. A few pages into each guys' life, and I realize what it's going to take to be a brilliant film actor . . . total insanity! I need to get crazy, and quick! Daniel Day-Lewis would truly become this homeless kid. He would walk in the character's shoes (that's done) and try to trick his mind into believing that this was his life. In his biography he's quoted as saying, "It's about really trying to imagine, discover, and attempting to create a world, an illusion of a world that other people might believe in because you believe in it yourself. It's a form of self-delusion." What did I tell you? Self-delusion=Crazy!

Marlon Brando's first movie part was playing this soldier who gets his legs blown off, so he checked himself into a veterans hospital and stayed in bed for a month! I need to find my character's loneliness and isolation. I have to stop hanging out with my family and friends and go live on the streets. I need to eat garbage and talk to myself more. I need to get dirty! When I tell C. B. my plan, he loves it; when I tell my parents, they're not as thrilled. They don't really understand this whole acting thing, either, but they don't want to get in my way, so they say it's okay to try one night at the Saur mansion.

I meet up with C. B. at the front gates, and he gives me a tour of the creepy old property. The red brick house is three stories with an observation tower on top. It's got five bedrooms, but C. B. used to sleep in the basement when he lived here. The whole yard is surrounded by tall cypress trees that don't allow anyone to see the grounds from the outside. Set decorators and construction guys are running around fixing up the house to get it ready for shooting. C. B. talks to one of the lighting guys, and I watch a crew build scaffolding around the sides of the house. They're probably trying to make sure that the wall doesn't fall down, but they may be preparing for the scene where my character is supposed to hang from the roof. I'm sure they'll have a stuntman do it, but I might be hanging/acting from that scaffolding. The thought freaks me out but excites me as well.

I get tired of waiting for C. B., and I walk into the scary basement by myself. My character lived in this damp, dark cave for almost two years. A chill goes down my spine as I pull the old lightbulb chain and it illuminates the crumbling stone foundation and rusted water pump. You can't see very far into the dark corners of the cellar, which is a relief because there has got to be some scary stuff back there. I know that I couldn't have done what C. B. did for real. There is a mattress on the ground, and I'm not sure if it's the same ratty-ass thing he used to sleep on or if it's a new one made up to look shabby. Either way, I'm not looking forward to sleeping on it. I try to suck it up and find courage. I close my eyes and try to channel my inner Daniel Day-Lewis. I breathe in the mildew and promptly cough. *Come on!* I imagine that I've been forced to live down here. I didn't choose it, but I bet I could live like a dirtbag, if I had to.

A scratching noise comes from under the stairs, so I step toward it but run into a spiderweb, scream like a bitch, and run the hell out of there, fast. I'm checking my hair for tarantulas, and shaking out the creeps, when I notice C. B. watching me. I try to spin my trembling into "actor preparation moves." He gives me an approving nod, and I walk around the property to explore the outbuildings (from a safe distance). I'm saying the lines out loud like a crazy person, but no one gives me a second look because I am an ACTOR! And we have permission, at all times, to be weird.

I find a half-eaten sandwich sitting on a tree stump and realize how hungry I am. If I'm getting into character, I can't just go down to Taco Bell; I have to eat trash to survive, and this sandwich is just sitting there, so I wolf it down. As I'm wiping my mouth with my shirt, wishing I had a drink, an art department guy with a bunch of tattoos comes out of the mansion and looks at the tree stump, before glaring at me as I swallow the last bite.

He asks, "Did you eat my lunch, you little—?"

I tell him I'm sorry, and C. B. sends some dude to a BBQ place to buy him another sandwich. I should tell the guy how the crew of *My Left Foot* had to carry Daniel Day-Lewis all around the set of that movie because his character couldn't walk, but I don't. Most people would be disappointed in me for eating a stranger's half-eaten food, but C. B. couldn't be more proud.

He wishes me luck with my research and says that he's got to go try and smooth things over with Ms. McDougle. She's still mad at him for throwing that party. I remind him to ask her plenty of questions: "Just because you drive a Ferrari doesn't mean you can skip the basics." It's weird giving a man advice to hook up with your teacher, but he's helping me out so much that I feel like I owe him. He offers up a high five before jumping into his car and barreling down the long driveway.

I've procrastinated long enough. It's time to try and walk around the upstairs part of the creepy, creaky, old mansion. It's ratty now, but you can see how nice it used to be, back in the day. I slowly make my way up into the third-floor turret to watch the sunset. I should be thinking about my character and how scary it must have been to live here, always worrying about someone finding you, and all of that drama, but I'm stuck on Abby and the stupid rocket-ship slide. What a dumbass! I watch the production crew unplug the generators at about nine thirty. All the lights go out, and they drive their trucks away. Here we go. It's time to dive into the research. I'm all alone . . . totally, completely, and utterly alone . . . I hope! The wind starts to blow the cypress trees around menacingly, and a wolf howls in the distance (may have been a border collie)! Why is it so dark in here all the sudden? I slowly fumble my way down the creaky stairs. I hear a door slam in one of the bedrooms, and

I quicken my pace. Something exhales on my neck, and I scream, "HAAAAHHH!"

Come on, man, it's just the wind. Quit bein' a puss! I shuffle into the kitchen and kick something soft. It's a dead body! No, it's a bag of sand with a handle. Friggin' crew guys! *Keep moving!* I slowly open the door to the basement, and a cold blast of musty wind hits me in the face. I turn to shut the door when a moaning sound bellows from behind me. *Keep moving!* I race down the rickety steps and jump on the old mattress. A cloud of dust flies into the air and makes me start coughing again. Good God! Something scurries out from under the box springs and heads toward the scratching noise coming from under the stairs. I imagine thousands of diseased rats tumbling on top of one another as a popping sound booms from upstairs. The only logical explanation: a monster has heard me and has emerged from his hiding place to come down and kill me.

I know I'm being a pussy, but I can't handle this. I rip open the basement door and fly out of the cellar. I grab my bike and race down the driveway at 9:35 p.m. I only made it five minutes, but research isn't always about quantity. And if my goal was to feel Chris's fear, then I'm good. And I'm not going directly home. There's a lot more to learn about being homeless than just sleeping in abandoned mansions, so I cruise around Merrian and pretend to be down and out for a couple more hours. I look for food in trash cans, but I don't eat any of it. I ride past Abby's house and see a police car up the road, so I ride away from it real fast. I'm kind of able to pretend that I'm on the run for real. I try not to have fun. I go back home and everyone is asleep, so I eat some leftover spaghetti. It's three days old, and I don't even heat it up (S'up, Brando?)! I head down to our basement to sleep on the couch. It isn't nearly as scary, unless you're frightened of eighties décor.

I've tried to avoid my family the past few days so I could feel what it would be like to lose them, but they're so annoying that they won't allow it. My dad comes down to the basement around two a.m. He sees I'm still awake and says, "I can't tell you how to be an actor, but I know you'll do a better job if you're rested."

"We start shooting in two days, and I just don't feel ready."

"Well, that's something I know about. You'll never feel completely *ready* for anything. Just do your best. You've worked hard, and that's all you can do. Sometimes you've just got to put up your sail and hope for wind."

"What the hell're you talkin' about, old man? We don't even have a boat."

He laughs and says, "You think I know how to build a deck?"

"Yeah."

He shrugs. "I don't. I got that book from Home Depot, but I've never really built anything. I'm just wingin' it."

"Remind me never to use the deck."

"You'll find that most people are just stumbling through. It's terrifying, but should be kind of inspiring for you to know that engineers, doctors, politicians . . . everybody is just using trial and error most of the time. We just keep moving forward until it becomes obvious that we should stop or turn around or whatever."

Eventually he goes up to bed, and I stop freaking out about the movie and start worrying about bridges collapsing, surgeries going bad, and international relations with China!

I only get two hours of sleep, but it doesn't matter that I'll be tired at rehearsal today, because part of the Saur mansion collapsed. I knew it! Goddamn freestylin' engineers! So Hilary and I get to rehearse for an extra week, and it takes some of the stress off of me. The problem is, Phil's anxiety has gone up and he's driving everyone nuts. His job is to keep everything on schedule, and I guess seven days is a big deal. Lynn is excited because she thinks she might get to do something besides steam clothes, but they just make her fetch coffee and food all day. . . . I love it.

We're rehearsing in an empty ballroom at the President Hotel. I guess Ms. McDougle has forgiven C. B., because she is at every rehearsal now, taking notes and asking us questions about our characters and figuring out if we know what we want from each moment. The ballroom is nice, but I wish we could work at the Saur mansion or one of the real locations. Matilda asked C. B. if we could do it here so it wouldn't disrupt Hilary's schedule too much. Usually he wouldn't listen to a bodyguard's suggestions, but he too is getting more stressed and therefore a bit more unpredictable. Hilary and I are having trouble acting the way he wants us to. I can tell he's frustrated, but I'm not sure how to make him happy. We just keep doing the scenes over and over, and McDougle grills us with question after question. Just last week C. B. asked me *not* to overwork the script and to just use "my instincts," so I'm a little confused but trying to roll with it. Hilary forgets the lines a lot, and C. B. gives her the note "Less Kidz Channel, please!" when she does a goofy double take or opens her mouth really wide with shock. You can tell she's pissed at him for dogging her, but she doesn't go off on him like she does Matilda or the assistants. She was raised doing that fake, overacting stuff, so it's hard for her to stop, but she's also a pro and makes the adjustment pretty well.

C. B. seems impressed by how prepared I am. He refers to my "raw talent" a few times, but I know that if I'd relied solely on that raw talent he would have thought he cast a retarded kid in his movie. We go over the crying scene a few times, but it doesn't go very well. I did so well at the audition, but I can't seem to get as angry or sad or disappointed or whatever it was I was feeling that day. He tells me not to sweat it, but I can tell he's starting to worry, and that makes me even more nervous. The script says it plain as day, "Chris breaks down. Maggie sobs."

After rehearsal one day, McDougle tells me I'm doing a really good job. It was supposed to be a compliment, but she said it with such surprise that I couldn't help but get a bit offended. And then, out of the blue, C. B. suggests that I start taking cold showers.

I ask him, "Have I been gawking? Do I need to raise my gaze?"

He laughs. "No, you're doing pretty good with that. The cold showers will help you get into the character, I think. See, I had to use that rusty pump in the basement, even in the winter. It'll make you appreciate hot water and the other blessings in your life like nothing else."

(I try it that night, and he's right, it sucks . . . and it really does help with horniness, too.)

* * *

During our extra week of rehearsal, I've had to make some adjustments to my "preparation." I've stopped running from the police, because a cop turned on his lights when I ran from him the other day, and I had to hide out in a Dumpster for twenty minutes. It was good research but I almost puked. It's bad to mix raw fear and rancid food.

The coolest thing to come from the rehearsals is that Hilary and I are really becoming friends. We've done Pilates again, and she introduced me to yoga and transcendental meditation. (It's really relaxing but almost more difficult than the physical working out, because most of the time I try so hard not to space out that's it's tough for me to do it on purpose.) We hang out at the mansion and watch the construction. They seem like they know what they're doing (most of the time). We eat take-out food and take long walks and talk about our characters. Matilda is never far away, and people will look at Hilary sometimes, but she doesn't acknowledge them, so they must think, No way. Why would Hilary Idaho be walking down the street in Merrian?

We tour my school and I show her all around. She's running up and down the halls like it's an amusement park and not a ratty old public high school. She wants to see my locker and all of the classrooms. She's bummed that the cafeteria isn't open for business, but I assure her that she is mistaken. "Just take your shoe off and try to eat it. That's about what the food is like."

I'm showing her the drama department on our way out to the parking lot. We cruise through the auditorium and I tell her about *Guys and Dolls* and how C. B. read to us from the book *Down Gets Out* in here.

She hops onto the stage and says, "Oh my God, that must have been so great for you guys!"

I nod that it was, but I've worked with Hilary just long enough to know when she's "acting," and she's not that impressed with *Guys and Dolls* or book readings. I don't see any reason to lie about it, though. I also don't see a need to call her on her BS, so we keep moving into the drama classroom. I was worried (hoping) that we would run into Abby and her College Carter Dumbass, but I guess the drama camp is on a field trip or something.

Matilda seems more comfortable the longer I'm around, and Hilary gets really upset when I try to leave. I know that there is no way that Hilary Idaho is into me, but if anyone else held my hand and kissed me on the cheeks and hugged me all the time the way she does . . . I'd have to think that they were *very* into me. Lynn was steaming clothes the other day and was watching Hilary and me goofing around. Hilary was flirting, saying how we need to rehearse the make-out scene, and getting really close to my face. Hilary was laughing, but I could see the wheels spinning inside my sister's head. She was trying to figure out what was going on; I don't think she came to any conclusions before she steamed her hand by accident and started screaming.

I haven't tried to sleep at the mansion again (because of the construction, not because I'm scared). But I have slept at the President Hotel a few times . . . in the living room area on the floor, of course. I pretend I'm stealing from the continental breakfast buffet. Hilary and her mom wake me up every morning by shouting at each other. It turns out I'm a light sleeper when I don't get to sleep on a bed. Her mom will usually yell, "You can't fire me, I'm your mother!" It really makes me appreciate the fact that my parents don't rely on me for their paychecks. My folks would be dead meat, and they would have fired me a long time ago.

I decide to sleep in my own bed the night before shooting starts, but I'm regretting it by dinnertime. I know that my family just wants to help me, and since I've been such a dumbass my whole life, they feel like they have to. But they're starting to piss me off. All they want to talk about is the movie, and I'm sick of it. I made the mistake of allowing them to help me work on the lines once, and they loved it so much that they want to rehearse all the time. I tell them to "give it a rest," but they still keep talking about the movie.

Mom wants Dad to wake up at five a.m. to drive me to the set, but I tell them that riding my bike will help me wake up and keep me from being too nervous. It will also seem cool to be the star of a movie and roll up on a Redline. She yells at me for wearing my ratty old Nikes when I have newer pairs, so I have to explain how Marlon Brando would change out of his character's costume but wouldn't take off the shoes, to stay connected to the character at all times.

She tells me, "I can smell them from across the room!" and we decide that Brando wouldn't object to a few shots of Febreze.

My dad wants to know why I keep rubbing my back all the time, and so I have to explain why I sleep on the floor now, and how Daniel Day-Lewis locked himself in a prison cell for months to get ready for a role. Dad doesn't understand how that would help an actor say his lines better, and I don't know how it's going to help either, but I'm *doing* it and I'm sick of TALKING ABOUT IT!

They beg me for one more rehearsal, and I don't have the heart to tell them no. We go over a few scenes in the living room, but my character is supposed to be pretty miserable, and they're laughing and carrying on like all of this work is sooo much fun. My dad is correcting me on the little details of the lines, and I'm not even supposed to have them memorized. My sister is reading Maggie's part, but she's doing an impression of Hilary when she does it and flipping her hair around. She's supposed to say this line, "Oh my God!" all serious when she sees that I got beaten up and thrown into a Dumpster, but my sister makes it all melodramatic and puts on a valley-girl accent, "Ohhh myyy GOD!"

I yell at them, "That's it, we're done! You people suck! In the future, if I want your help, I will ask for it!"

I'm down in the basement going over the crying scene again. I'm not sad but I'm so frustrated that I feel like I could burst into tears at any moment, but when I actually try to use it . . . nothing! We don't shoot this thing for a few weeks, but it's stressing me. What if I can't cry? What if C. B. calls "action" and I just scrunch up my face and go, "Boo, hoo!" He'll kick the crap out of me for wrecking his film. Sport Coat Phil will probably sue my family for "failure to weep."

If I just keep looking at it, it'll come to me. I'll magically figure out what to do if I concentrate hard enough and focus on something sad. I'm taking deep breaths and saying the lines out loud, but I'm thinking about my grandma's funeral and how sad my mom was that day. Grandma was old, but Mom seemed really surprised when she finally kicked. I'm sure my mom was thinking about old times, like when her mom made her prom dress or baked her cakes. I seem to remember her getting really pissed off at Grandma all the time and yelling at her for buying Lynn and me toys or trying to clean our house when Mom was at work. Maybe she was feeling regret for not being nicer. Maybe she yelled at her mom the day before she bit it. Eventually this line of thinking leads me to consider that my mom will die someday. And how she won't always be around to nag me. For some reason, that is a very sad thought. I look around the basement and think about a time when I'll have to come down here and clean all this crap out. This is where we store all the junk that's no longer fit to show people. The plastic Christmas tree lives down here under the shelves of old books. Lynn's and my framed artwork is all over the place. It used to be cute for people to look at when we were little, but started to get a little pathetic in the past few years. Somebody might get the idea that I'd just done one of these finger paintings and think, Something is goofed up with that Carter boy. I chuckle to myself, but soon find warm tears streaming down my cheeks. I reach for the script while looking at the box of stuffed animals that will wind up in a Dumpster someday. . . . *Oh, Snoopy!* I try to say a few of the lines, but it's hard for me to talk. I'm so sad. *Tinky-Winky! Old friend!* Just as I start to pull myself together and find the balance between blubbering and talking, the basement door flies open and my sister bounds down the stairs to yell at me.

"Why are you being such a dick to Mom and Dad?!"

I draw the script over my head and slam it down on an old chest. Dust flies into the air as I scream, "UUAAAAAHHHHHHH!!! Damn it!" The pages scatter.

She looks totally shocked by my reaction, so I clarify. "I'm trying to do something down here!"

She asks, "What's your problem?"

"I'm *trying* to concentrate and get into character. And in case you haven't noticed, I'm under a lot of pressure, and you people will not leave me alone! Get off my nuts!"

She crosses her arms and glares at me. She knows that bitchiness runs in our family, but she's never seen it in me before. She's not sure if she wants to push her agenda or start cheering.

She simply, pathetically says, "We're just trying to help."

"So please do, and leave me alone!"

In shock, she turns and walks back upstairs.

God, these people! I can't find the sadness again, but anger is ready to roll whenever I need to tap into it.

14. ACTION!

It's technically morning when I take a fast freezing-cold shower and ride out of the driveway at five fifteen a.m. I guess nobody told the sun I was getting up this early. It's still pitch-black when I take the shortcut behind Pizza Barn, and I decide not to take the jump. I wish I'd been able to sleep more, but I was just too fired up. This is probably why actors get into drugs. One pill to sleep, one to wake up, one to unwind, one to laugh, one to cry, and then you die on the toilet when you're thirty. If they have any Cokes on the set, I'll probably slam one. Caffeine was probably Heath Ledger's gateway, too.

The world is orange when I roll up to the set . . . fifteen minutes early! The mansion is surrounded by trucks and RVs. The house isn't nearly as scary with all of these people bustling around. The crew guys are setting up lights and running wires into the basement as if they don't mind monsters or rats. I ride up and give a nod to the guy I stole the sandwich from. He's plugging cables into a generator and doesn't return the nod, so I just keep looking for the Cokes.

I'm warming up my voice and stretching, because that's what actors do, when a Merrian cop car pulls into the gravel driveway. I recognize the guy from the D.A.R.E. program at my school, but I'm already so into character that

I take off running. The cop must be perplexed as to why I did that, because he grabs his billy club and hops out of the car.

In a deep cop voice he yells, "HEY!!!" and the entire crew stops what they're doing, except me. I just keep running.

After ducking behind the production trailer, I'm able to calm down for a second and ask myself, "What the hell are you doing, you dumbass?"

The cop is jogging toward me when I step out from behind the RV, throw my hands up, and say, "Sorry about that, dude, I didn't mean to freak you out. I'm just trying to get into—"

He interrupts. "What do you think you're doing?"

I smile with pride and reply, "Well, I-I-I'm starrin' in this movie."

He puts his club in its holster and laughs. "Yeah, me too."

"Really?" I ask. (I've read the script a hundred times—could I have missed a cop character?)

"Yeah, I'm playing the police officer."

"Huh? I didn't even realize—"

He interrupts me again. "My first line is: 'This is a closed set, boy.' And then I say, 'Get the hell out of here!'"

"Man, I just don't remember—"

He barks, "Beat it, before I cuff and stuff your ass!"

Being a movie star doesn't give you as much clout as I'd hoped. "I-I-I'm the star of this movie . . . seriously."

"Sure ya are," he says, marching toward me. "Two choices! Go home, or go to jail."

I back away from him and stutter, "D-Dude, dude . . . okay, I'm not technically *the star*, but I've got a lot of lines!"

He grabs my shirt and asks, "So we're gonna have to do this the hard way?"

"I guess we are, 'cause I'm not—"

I'm on my face before I can finish the statement. Grass is up my nose as the cold steel cuffs lock my wrists together. All of these crew bastards are just watching the show, like they've worked with Robert Downey Jr. too many times and it's natural to see their lead actor getting arrested on the first day of shooting.

Thank God, the Ferrari roars onto the set as I'm being stuffed into the back of the squad car. C. B. jumps out with his sunglasses on and cell phone pressed to his ear. He yells, "Sorry I'm late, guys!"

Son of a bitch! He didn't even notice me.

"C. B.!!!" I yell.

The cop responds, "Shut it, kid!"

"Ceee-Beee!!!" I yell as the door slams in my face.

Finally he turns and lowers his shades before asking, "Carter?"

"YEAH!!!" I shout at the thick glass.

I barely hear the cop ask, "You know this kid, Mr. Down?"

"Yeah, he's the lead actor in our movie. . . . What did he do?"

I'm out of the car and the cuffs are off of me in an instant as the cop responds, "Nothing, I guess. He was just lippin' off and took off running when I drove up. . . . It's not the first time either. He's ridden away from me a few times this week, like he's up to something."

C. B. smiles like a proud parent and explains, "Yeah, we think he's the next Daniel Day-Lewis."

The cop smiles and slyly adds, "Yeah, or Sean Penn."

Sport Coat Phil and his assistant walk up and yell at me to start getting ready. C. B. throws his arm around my shoulder and says, "Come on, ya menace, let's get you into hair and makeup."

We step up into the beauty shop on wheels, and he introduces me to all the ladies who casually watched me getting "cuffed and stuffed" a few minutes ago. They toss their issues of *US Weekly, People,* and *Star* magazines on the counter and fawn all over me. I've gone from the scum of the earth to the most important guy on the planet because I walked in with the right person. This is the clout I was looking for!

As they hose me down and make me up, C. B. explains, "We were going to start with interior shots. But I've heard Hilary is going to be running late . . . every day, so we might try to sneak in the scene where you break into the house for the first time. You wanna smash out a window?"

"Hell, yeah," I reply, and C. B. walks out of the trailer to get set up.

A lady hands me an *US Weekly* and starts to wash all the "notes to self" off my arms. I start to yell, "I NEED THOSE!!!" but hold it in. I'm not retarded. I know all my lines, and I even made it here early today. The scribbles may be like Dumbo's lucky feather, and it's time to let them go.

They put anti-gel in my hair to make it look unwashed, and touch up my bruises with brushes and sponges. In the movie my character keeps getting into fights, so the wounds from my bike wreck work perfectly for some scenes, but not others.

The makeup lady explains why she's making me cry.

"We've got to make your injuries look the same every day."

I'm guessing that this chick has read some of those acting books that say, "You must suffer for your craft!" because she's poking at my wounds with a sharp pencil. I'm trying not to move, but my nervous system has a mind of its own, and it keeps dodging the blows.

"Hold still!" she demands.

"Sorry . . . th-th-those are actual cuts and bruises, you know?"

She sighs without compassion, because C. B. is gone, and says, "Quit being a bitch," like one of my boys.

That's not cool, we just met! I take the pain for six hundred and twelve more seconds by focusing on the latest Hollywood gossip and accidentally ripping out all the pages of *US Weekly*. Tears are shooting out of my eyes when she rips a scab off of my ear, then decides that she liked it better before and starts to draw it back on. I spring from the chair and bark, "You gotta be kiddin' me!?"

She looks pissed, but motions that I'm free to go.

I'm sitting on a tree stump, trying to get back into character and regain the feeling in my face, when Phil walks up and puts on a plastic smile. "Hey, buddy!"

I nod. "S'up?"

"You ready to shoot your first scene in a Hollywood movie?"

"Hollywood? I thought this was a Merrian film." He doesn't laugh, so I say, "Sorry, yeah, you want me to break a window?"

He awkwardly tries to give me a high five and says, "You got it! You're a step ahead of me already. You're just going to walk up to that basement door, look around to see if the coast is clear, and then smash out the glass with a rock. Then you unlock the door and walk inside . . . Piece of cake, pal!"

I may be wrong about needing those "notes to self" and not being retarded, because this guy is positively talking to a retarded person . . . and he's addressing his comments to me.

I'm trying to think of something smart to say, but nothing is coming. C. B. asks for me to come over to where he has the camera set up, and yells at Phil, "Quit talking to the actors!"

The sun has finally come up, but they have the old cellar door lit anyway. The crew guy, whose sandwich I ate, gives me a nod as he adjusts a light. I nod back.

C. B. looks up from his camera and tells the guy, "You're in frame," and he moves his light again. Then C. B. asks me, "You ready to try one?"

I nod and smile, but I can't speak and my hands are shaking all the sudden. He takes my response to mean that I am *not* ready to try one, so he says, "That's fine, bro. We're just keepin' it loose. It's okay to be nervous. Let's just rehearse one for camera. You know what you're doing?"

I violently nod that I do, so he announces, "Okay, just a walk-through, people! Half speed. Carter's going to pantomime the motion with the rock and the entrance to the house. This is MOS, camera ready, and—"

I yell, "Wait . . . I'm sorry. What am I doing with the rock? And I don't know what MOS is!"

I see Phil shake his head out the corner of my eye. C. B. responds, "MOS just means we're not recording sound, so nobody has to be quiet. And you're just showing us what you're going to do with the rock."

I softly try to clarify, "Throw it, right?"

He doesn't hear me, and yells, "Rehearsal's up! Ready? And Carter . . . ACTION!"

I bust out laughing. Dang it! I've heard movie director's yell "ACTION" a million times on TV and stuff, but it's never been directed at me. C. B. looks up from his camera, annoyed. He shows me his knuckle tattoos and grunts, "Stay focused." I jump up and down and shake my head around, trying to pull myself together before reaching down and opening the cellar doors. I think about how hard it is to live on the streets, totally exposed to the elements, and how much better life would be if I could get inside that basement. Yeah, I'm feeling it! I look around before pulling the biggest, heaviest piece of concrete out of the crumbling wall. I draw it behind my head like a soccer ball and heave it with an "Uhhh!" *CRASH!!!* The glass smashes into a million pieces. I'm not sure if they want me to go into the basement or not, so I look back at C. B. to see. It seems like something is wrong. He and the rest of the crew look shocked.

Phil yells at me, "Idiot! You broke the damn window!"

I ask, "Huh?"

C. B. jumps up from the camera and barks, "Shut up, Phil!"

He retorts, "The kid obviously has no experience. . . . We're dead meat. The studio is going to pull the plug!"

C. B. pushes Phil backward, and seethes, "If you break my actor's confidence, I'll kill you! Got it?"

I look at the crew guy and whisper, "Wasn't I supposed to break the glass?"

He replies, "Yeah, but we were just rehearsing, so you were just supposed to pantomime."

"Ohhh, *pantomime*!" I cringe.

He explains, "We have three other windows, so don't sweat it. Producers are just bitches about money." He points a gloved finger to the lights, and explains, "A movie set like this breaks down to roughly a thousand dollars a minute. It'll take us about twenty to replace the window, so you just cost him twenty grand, is all."

Dang it. As they clean up my expensive mistake, C. B. comes over and tells me that I did a great job and not to listen to Phil and not to look at the camera next time. He sets up his shot and then comes back over to give me a pep talk. "You want inside that house, man. You're on the run, you're desperate and hungry. This house is going to save you. Everything you've ever wanted and need is in there. Can you imagine that?"

I nod that I can, so he calmly says, "Okay, let's roll this one. Camera ready . . . Speed?"

A big guy with headphones on yells back, "Speeding!"

I don't stop to ask what that means, because C. B. says, "Carter . . . action when you're ready."

I don't laugh this time and I'm not ready, so I jump up and down a few more times and think about what I want more than anything. What is this perfect thing that's going to make my life complete, the ideal that's just on the other side of that door? I think about Ferraris . . . *Playboy* centerfolds . . . armored trucks filled with money . . . and then, for some reason (ADD), my mind drifts to an image of Abby inside that basement. She's wearing roller skates, and she's laughing at me.

I hear Phil mutter, "For the love of God," as I fling the cellar doors open and descend the stairs to look through the new glass on the old door. Inside, I can still see broken shards on the floor. With all the lights behind me I can also see myself in the reflection and the fear in my eyes, and I can hear Abby's laughter ringing in my ears. She thinks I'll screw this up, just like I did the dress rehearsal. . . . Everybody thinks I will. I may be looking into the eyes of the only person who thinks I won't. I look back to the yard and pick up my rock. I take a deep breath and close my eyes to channel the anger. I reach it back and yell, "Shut UP!" before throwing the rock with all of my might. I hear a loud *CRUNCH* instead of the *CRASH* I was expecting. The rock misses the glass and smashes into the wooden part of the old door, splintering it into a thousand pieces and knocking it completely off its frame. Dang it. It's still hanging by the top hinge, so I finish it off with a kick and walk over it as I step inside the basement. Then I dumbly pick it up and try to push it back into the opening . . . like nobody is going to notice this bazillion-dollar screwup! "No problem, people. Carter's fixed it!" I step to the side of the door and softly beat my head against the stone wall.

I hear C. B. yell, "CUT!" and wonder what the record is for how fast an actor was fired off of a movie.

The first face I see is that of the pissed-off crew guy when he lifts the door out of his way and stomps into the basement to assess the damages. His expression suggests that this is a bigger goof up than eating his lunch, and although they had a couple more pieces of glass for me to break, they don't have any more door frames.

Everyone is staring at me as I walk up the steps toward the camera. Phil is holding his head in his hands, but C. B. is smiling at me like I just gave him a puppy. He exclaims, "What'd I tell you about this kid's instincts?! Marlon friggin' Brando! Brilliant! If he breaks the glass, someone would notice, and it would let the cold air in during the winter! So he takes out the frame and puts it back! I wish I'd thought of it. Check the gate! That was perfect!"

Man, I want this guy around all the time to spin my screwups into "brilliant, perfect instincts." I guess we're done with that shot because an assistant takes me to an RV and tells me to hang out until they need me again. The door shuts and I immediately collapse to the floor. Oh my God, this is sooo STRESSFUL!!!

15. WINO

I'm not sure how long I was asleep when Hilary knocks on the door. In a fog, I open it and she walks in with a bathrobe on and curlers in her hair.

"Hey," I say.

"Good morning," she says, walking into the kitchen area and pulling a Diet Coke out of a mini-fridge. "Sorry I'm late."

It's my first day of filming the lead part in a movie. I'm alone in a trailer with an international superstar wearing a skimpy robe, and all I can think to say is, "Whoa, we have Cokes!"

She slides up onto the countertop and tells me that her mom got bored and went back to L.A. last night. She says that she's glad she left, but I can tell she's bummed.

I awkwardly ask, "Merrian was too much for her, huh?"

She looks out the window and sighs, "If I didn't have to be stuck here, I guess I'd leave too."

She's fidgeting and doesn't seem right this morning, so I ask, "You okay?"

She tells me that she's just amped up because she's nervous. She really wants to do a good job on the scenes today and prove to the world that she's a serious actress. Like me, she wants C. B. to see how great she can be.

I tell her what my mom told me as I was rolling out this morning: "You just have to relax and be yourself. Everybody loves you. You're special, and you're gonna be great!"

She shakes her hands around frantically, and angrily says, "Well, I'm trying!"

Mom also told me to take a deep breath, so I give her that one too. She does, but I can see her chest trembling as she inhales. I got a hug as well, so I pull Hilary off the counter and give her a good squeeze. I rock her back and forth a few times until she starts laughing, and I say, "Better? Good."

She looks up at me with a smile, and we get a bit more serious. I may not be a Cassanova playa but I know a green light when I see it. Intellectually, I know that there is no way that this chick should be into me, but I know that look and she wants to kiss me! So I whisper, "You wanna work on the make-out scene?"

She leans in closer, closes her eyes and sighs, "Sure," but just as our lips are about to meet, I catch a whiff of her breath. The "Sure" puffs out like a cloud, and it stinks . . . like alcohol.

My head automatically tilts back. Dang it, has she been drinking . . . at nine a.m.? I should be really turned on right now. This a very sexy situation, but I'm totally upset. I don't want to flip out or seem like a choirboy, but I do not want to kiss her either. She seems aware of my stiffness and probably wonders why I've left her hanging.

She asks, "What's wrong?"

I smell it again and I try not to make a face. I could be wrong, and I don't want to accuse her of anything, so I say, "I-I-I'm just not sure if we should, you know? It's the first time our characters kiss. It might be better to save this moment for the camera."

She nods as her mind races. She looks angry but then decides not to be. She kind of slurs, "Sure, sure, sure. You are sooo right, Carter!" and kisses me on the cheek.

I reply, "I-I-I'm all about character!" as the door to the trailer flies open.

Matilda's head bursts in just as Hilary's lips are pulling away from my face. The trailer shakes as Matilda steps up and pushes me away from her client. "I can't leave you alone for five minutes!"

As Hilary's being dragged out the door, she shoots me an embarrassed smile.

I tell her, "Don't worry about it, my mom might fly through that door any minute and bust me for having soda this early." The door slams and I try to laugh it off, but I need to sit down. I feel sick. Why would anyone get up in the morning and have a cocktail, especially Hilary Idaho? My boys have started drinking at parties, but I don't think they hop out of bed and crack a beer. And this feels worse to me because Hilary has been to rehab. So she's made a real effort to not use drugs or alcohol. I wonder if I should tell someone? Do they already know and not care? Her mom is out of the picture, and C. B. and Phil would flip out from the additional pressure, and Matilda would pull the plug on the whole movie. Am I looking out for Hilary or am I being selfish? Am I just using her like everyone else? I really want to talk to Abby.

Of course, when I step outside, she's standing about fifty feet away from my trailer, and I immediately lock eyes with her. She's standing next to the lighting guys, who

are rushing around getting ready for Hilary's and my first scenes. I'm so surprised and happy to see her that I forget about Hilary for a second and wave to her like a total idiot. "Abby! Hey!" If you can't be cool when you're starring in a movie, when can you? She only gives me a nod because the camera guy is holding a tape measure to her chin. He's trying to figure out his focus, and she's trying to ignore me and do her job. She's all lit up beside the broken basement door. She looks so professional and sooo hot!

Hilary bounds out of her trailer a few minutes later, and she seems much better. She asks me, "Are you ready to shoot?"

I look at her suspiciously because she seems to have a lot more energy. She leans in to ask, "Are you okay?"

Her breath wafts into my nostrils after her "okay" and it smells like freshly added Listerine. I start acting a few minutes before the cameras roll by smiling and saying, "I'm great, let's do it!"

She grabs my hand and tells me not to be nervous. Abby pretends that she doesn't notice who I'm holding hands with.

Our first scenes go pretty well. It's after I've broken into the house and she's watched me crawling under the fence. She follows me inside the basement. They do a bunch of shots of us almost running into each other and me hearing a noise, and then we scare the crap out of each other in the doorway to the basement. We do some walking shots, and that's not as easy as it looks! I had decided that when I tell her what happened to my parents, I wanted to try to cry a little bit, but C. B. can see what I'm doing and he knows it's forced. He yells "CUT!" and looks up from the camera before he seethes, "Keep it real."

I try to forget about Hilary's breath, and I'm so glad we've been able to hang out like we have, because the characters are supposed to be friends. I'm still able to joke around with her, and I think it adds a layer to our friendship, now that I know how truly screwed up she is.

C. B. was right about doing the scenes a million times. It takes all day to shoot a little nothing-type scene. They shoot us from every angle you can think of. The crew guys tweak things a thousand times before they decide it's right. They recheck their light meters and raise their gel stands a half an inch and lower them a sixteenth; they play with the microphones and boom poles every chance they get. You'd think that shadows or camera angles had the ability to make or break a movie, the way everyone worries about them. I think they're all just trying to look busy. I do stuff like that a lot, so I can spot it. If you're talking loud and hustling all over the place, who would dare accuse you of being a slacker?

At about six thirty p.m., Matilda tells Phil's assistant to tell Phil to tell C. B. that Hilary has worked for eight hours and fifty-five minutes, and if they go ten minutes longer, she'll call the starlet's union and they'll slap them with a child labor suit that will shut the movie down. We're just about to shoot our first scene inside the house. It takes place during a thunderstorm, and the guys have just figured out how much rain to shoot onto the windows and how much lightning they can flash without it looking fake, but C. B. has to wrap for the day, and he's pissed. I should point out that I started three hours before Hilary, and I'm actually younger, but it doesn't seem like anyone would care, so I don't.

I wash off my makeup bruises to let the real ones

breathe. I remove my costume Levi's and T-shirt to put on my own for the ride home. I'm just hopping on my bike when I see Abby walking out of one of the RVs. I really want to talk to her about Hilary's booze breath this morning and what she thinks I should do, but since we haven't hung out in such a long time, I don't think I should just bombard her with my issues, so I hit her with a warm-up question. "Uh, how are you doing?"

She doesn't stop to talk to me, though. She just keeps walking, and mutters, "I'm fine."

I reply, "Great, great, so standing is okay. . . . Being a stand-in is going good, then?"

She's directly in front of Hilary's trailer when she stops and turns toward me (questions are so awesome). Unfortunately, Matilda is guarding the door and listening to our every word, so I'll have to move this conversation if I'm going to get into the Hilary situation.

But all Abby's able to say is, "Yeah, it's not too—" before Hilary flies out of the RV and interrupts our first chat in weeks by yelling, "Carter!"

We both turn to see Hilary bounding out of the trailer, followed closely by Sport Coat Phil. Hilary gives me a couple winks before she asks, "Where are we having dinner again?"

I look at Abby, who raises her eyebrows. Ms. McDougle's first rule of impov is, "Never deny." So no matter what the other actor gives you, you just have to roll with it. I'm pretty good at improv, so I calmly tell her, "Uh, weee . . . are going to eat at . . . my house?"

She smiles and says, "Perfect, I'd forgotten." Then she jumps on my pegs like we weren't pretending. Did I invite her to dinner and space it? I've never asked anyone to "have dinner," so I doubt I'd forget. She theatrically yells to Phil and Matilda, "Yeah, so, I'm going to eat with Carter's family, for research!"

Phil gives me a suspicious look, along with Matilda and Abby. How is this my fault . . . whatever *this* is?

Hilary smiles at Abby, then asks me, "Will your friend be joining us?"

I reply, "Uhhh—"

But Abby interrupts. "No."

"Have you guys not met?" I ask. "Hilary this is my— uh, Abby."

Pretty bitchily and almost in unison, they reply, "We've met."

Abby looks slightly wounded when she says, "I'll just see you guys tomorrow. . . . Have a good dinner," and then walks down the driveway.

I watch her go and wait for the Escalade to fire up before rolling out. I guess I don't really need Abby's help. I make a right turn out of the driveway and pedal toward my house. Maybe I can find my own way to talk to Hilary.

We ride in silence for a while before I ask, "S'up?"

I was trying to ask her about her substance abuse problems, but my question may have been a little too open-ended. She tells me that Sport Coat Phil was just giving her a lecture in the trailer when she saw me ride by. "You totally saved me! Phil is so annoying."

I really want to ask her what he was lecturing her about, and why her breath smelled like a wino's this morning, but I chicken out and just explain that she's having "breakfast for dinner" tonight. "It sounds weird, but we always do it on Tuesdays and it's really good. It's just, like, waffles and scrambled eggs."

She giggles. "Sounds awesome, I can't wait."

"Yeah, my mom always makes extra food so my dad can take it to work the next day. . . . He won't mind if Hilary Idaho eats his lunch."

We take the shortcut behind Pizza Barn, and I describe my bike wreck in all of its gory detail. I may exaggerate a bit, but she seems entertained. I know that I'm talking too much, and I should be asking more questions, but everything that pops into my mind today is really negative. Finally I ask, "Hey, did Matilda really make you take a drug test when you got home the other day?"

She ignores the real question, and replies, "That's not my home. It's just a hotel room and a bodyguard."

I look back at the Escalade on our heels and say, "I think Matilda really cares about you."

She scoffs, "It's her job. She gets paid for that, you know?"

I feel like Matilda's job is just to protect her from stalkers, but I don't say it.

16. SUGAR-FREE PUDDING

We walk into the house and I can smell waffles burning. My mom's not around, and I can hear Lynn yapping on the phone, obviously ignoring her cooking duties. I lift the lid and crunch a fork into the smoking black squares. "You like 'em well done, yeah?"

Hilary laughs as I throw them in the trash. I pour more batter into the cooker and ask Hilary to keep an eye on them. "When the light turns green, eject 'em."

She gives me a thumbs-up as I walk into the living room and wave to get my sister's attention. "Hey."

"On the phone, dickhead!" Lynn replies.

I motion for her to lower her voice, and whisper, "Hilary Idaho is having dinner with us."

"What?" she asks. "Hang on. My super-important movie star brother is telling me something about Hilary Idaho, and I need to take notes."

I shake my fist at her and whisper, "No . . . she's having dinner here . . . with us."

Lynn scrunches up her face and barks, "Who is? I can't understand you when you mumble!" She says into the phone, "Yeah, he thinks he's friggin' Marlon Brando."

I whisper as slowly and clearly as I can, "Hil-ar-y Id-a-ho is—"

"Yes, Hil-ary Id-a-ho-BAG . . . I got it . . . and you're a rock star because you've talked to that skinny, fake bitch? I'm ooon the phooo—"

Her words trail off and her eyes double in size when Hilary walks into the living room with two waffles on a fork and says, "Carter, I need a plate for these."

I nod my head judgmentally at Lynn, and mouth the words "Nice job" before walking back into the kitchen.

I compliment Hilary on her grill skills. "You could get a job at Waffle House if the movie star thing doesn't pan out."

Hilary laughs, and my dad stomps in the front door from work, tosses his briefcase on the table, and asks, "Who's that big momma out in the Escalade?"

I throw my hands up and sigh, "Please!!! Be cool."

My dad is not one to be told what to do, so he makes a goofy face, hunches over, and puts on a goofy voice when he says, "Ohhh, so sorry, I'm not cool enough to *hang* with your friends, Will. Hello, young lady. I'm Carter's dorky dad . . . and what's your name?"

I shake my head and gasp. "Daaad, this is my costar."

He sticks out his hand for her to shake and says, "Sorry, I don't know what a *coaster* is, either."

She lets go of his hand when she realizes that he's not kidding around. He really has no idea who she is. I tell her, "He lives in a cave and sometimes forgets who I am, so don't be offended."

She mumbles, "It's okay," and removes the next batch of waffles.

My mom plays it cool (thank God). She just welcomes her to our house and tells her she's doing a great job with the waffles. She's cracking eggs for her famous (not) "trash-can scramble" when Nick Brock slams the front door and stomps into the kitchen covered in dirt. He yells his usual greeting. "S'up, Carter family?"

Mom swings the spatula at him and barks, "Dirty boots, off!"

He sits on a chair and is untying his Red Wings when I ask him, "How is your construction job going?"

"It sucks a fat one. How's the movie?"

My mom smacks his shoulder and dust flies into the air. Hilary lets out a giggle as Nick gets up and leaves a mud print of his butt on the chair. He gives her a sideways look and asks, "Heeey, don't I know you?!"

She smiles proudly in the hopes that someone will start to properly kiss her ass around here, but Nick continues, "Yeah, you cut grass for Harding Landscape, don't you?"

Her expression shifts to disgust. "No, I do not *cut grass*."

My sister bursts into the room to save the day: "NICK, this is Hilary Idaho!"

"Yeah, yeah, I know that name too. . . . You're not a weed eater?"

Hilary pulls a couple more waffles out and mutters, "No, no I am not."

"Gravel girl?"

Lynn is looking at him like he's kicking the dog. Hilary has checked out of the conversation and is pouring batter with all of her focus when Nick wraps his massive arms around her shoulders, lifts her off the ground and laughs, "I'm just messin' with you, Hilary! I was a *Get Up Gang* member in eighth grade!"

I laugh with everybody else at the thought of this all-American linebacker watching tween TV and joining a fan club, until he throws up the *Get Up Gang* sign and Hilary returns the corresponding finger move, and they shout in unison, "G.U.G. fo' life, baby!"

Lynn grabs my arm during the second round of laughs and quietly tells me, "If you tell anyone about this, I'll kill you."

"Who would believe me?"

The doorbell rings and my dad lets Matilda in the front door. Her jaw is flexed and she stares Nick Brock down, before saying, "No touching."

Nobody tells Nick what to do, so he asks, "Excuse me?"

"I'd prefer it if you didn't make physical contact with Ms. Idaho."

Nick is as embarrassed as Hilary when he says, "Yeah, sure . . . I'm . . . sor—"

Hilary screeches, "Matilda, get the hell out of here and stop embarrassing me!"

The mood is very tense until my mom asks Matilda to stay for dinner. Hilary pulls out more waffles and snidely says, "You're going to need a lot more batter."

As we start eating, my dad asks Matilda what she does, and she cheerfully replies, "I'm an armed, legal body guardian."

We all kind of stiffen and think about the "armed" part of her job description. But Lynn is very interested in new careers, because being an assistant to the assistant costume designer is not as fun as she thought. She asks, "What does that mean?"

Matilda replies, "I'm a legal representative for Hilary, like a parent . . . but I'm also authorized to shoot people if they threaten her safety."

Everyone is staring at her, waiting for her to smile and tell us that she's joking, but the smile never comes.

My sister excitedly asks, "Do you have to go to school for that?"

Hilary answers, "No, any idiot can do it; you just have to get lucky."

Matilda smoothly says, "Or unlucky."

"Oh, that's a burn," I add.

Hilary smiles and playfully pushes me. "Shut up, Carter."

Nick keeps us laughing through dinner by making fun of my mom and singing his version of "Go! Fight! Win!" Hilary howls with laughter when I join him for the "Weeeeiiiiieeauuuna!" She's not used to people dogging her to her face, and she seems to love it. My life would be a lot easier if I enjoyed it more.

Matilda gives Hilary the death stare when she puts her knife into the butter tub, and takes the syrup out of her hands before she can flip the lid. I try to eat mine dry, too, but it sucks, so I sneak some syrup when she's not looking. Hilary only eats two bites of eggs, and half a waffle. My dad tries to take the other half off her plate, but my mom shoots the action down with her own death stare.

We finish, and everybody is clearing their dishes. Matilda tries to clear Hilary's plate, but puts it down when she realizes that Hilary wants to do it herself. As my mom is loading the dishwasher she tells everyone about our family rehearsals. I'm red with embarrassment until Hilary asks if she can join in.

Matilda says it would be okay and asks if she can read the stage directions. My dad hands her his script like it's no big deal, but she seems really excited to get the job. Shockingly, I know all of my lines. Even my sister is impressed as I rattle them off. I sit on the floor because my character doesn't own chairs. Hilary sits down next to me. The third scene we work on is the one that we were supposed to shoot this afternoon inside the mansion. Hilary/Maggie asks me why I won't play sports, go to parties, or do anything fun anymore.

I/Chris think about the answer for a second, then shrug. "'Those things seem silly to me now, I guess. It was my mom . . . She always wanted me to play sports so I'd fit in, and she bought me nice clothes. I really thought I cared about all that . . . but now it doesn't matter.'"

Hilary/Maggie asks if I miss having a mom, and I begin my biggest monologue in the script: "'I still have a mom. She takes me shopping at Target about once a week and she buys me anything I want and we walk out with, like, twenty bags of stuff and she's so happy. I've had the dream about fifty times now, and I've figured out that when we reach the parking lot, it's about over, so I put down the stuff and try to give my mom a hug and thank her, but I never get to do it and I always wake up crying. It's funny because the muscles in my face hurt the next day from smiling so much during the dream. I really do try to be happy, because I know that's what she'd want, but it's hard.'"

I wasn't trying to deliver a performance or anything. I was just trying to say the words in the right order because it's a lot to remember, but I did it almost perfect. Out of the corner of my eye, I see that my mom has started crying.

A tear rolls down Hilary's cheek as she reads, "'We can work on that, but I wasn't talking about clothes. I'm talking about fun—'"

I interrupt her. "'I have fun with you.'"

"'What would your mom say if she knew that the only time you smiled was when you were asleep?'" she asks with real compassion. She's a much better actor without all of the producers and cameras around.

I just look at her for a second and shake my head. I'd like to say the next line quietly, but my mom is openly blubbering, so I have to turn up the volume when I say, "'She wouldn't like it, but she'd like you.'"

Matilda reads, "'Maggie passionately kisses Chris.'"

Hilary looks at me intensely, like she might. I'm into the scene, but I'm still aware that my parents are in the room and her body guardian is "armed."

Nick saves me by jeering, "Go for it!" and everyone laughs.

The next scene allows my sister to read the part of Maggie's friend, who thinks my character is a dirtbag, so she's having way too much fun flicking her hair around before reading, "'He probably has lice!'"

Nick plays the principal of the school with a funny deep voice. He tells me that although he enjoyed my essay, he had to call social services. Hilary asks him with disgust, "'How could you?'"

It's a sad and serious scene. I'm supposed to be depressed but also relieved that I don't have to be homeless anymore. Nick is done with his lines, but he jumps up and yells, "Do not question the PRINCIPAL!!! I have absolute power!" The scene turns into a *Saturday Night Live* sketch when he picks me up and starts tossing me around the room. Everyone is cracking up.

After about an hour, we've done most of the script. The crying scene was a bit wonky because Hilary did her fake crying, and Nick thought she was trying to be funny and so he started fake crying, too. It pulled me out of the scene, and Hilary seemed pretty embarrassed. Matilda picked up the slack and started reading the next scene, so Hilary couldn't stay down for very long.

We run through tomorrow's scenes twice, and finally Matilda says, "Fade to black."

Nick adds, "That's it?"

Lynn asks Hilary, "Isn't it too short to be a movie?"

Hilary says, "No, this is actually really long. You should read the crap I usually work on. We'd have been at a club doing shots by now!"

Everyone just looks at her. That joke may fly in Hollywood, but at the Carter house it goes over like the time my mom tried to sneak sugar-free pudding into her cream puffs.

Matilda clears her throat angrily and gives the script back to my dad. "We should go. Hilary needs to do cardio and tan before bed."

Brock tries to lighten the vibe by stretching and saying, "Whew, me too," but nobody laughs.

Hilary is embarrassed and clarifies, "I was joking."

I make a face, like "It's not a big deal," and offer up a high five before saying, "So, I'll see you at the butt crack of dawn?"

She halfheartedly returns the five and tells my mom goodnight before following Matilda to the SUV. We all watch from the kitchen window as Matilda shuts Hilary's door and they drive off. Mom mutters, "Poor thing."

Lynn scoffs, "Whatever, she's a bazillionaire."

Dad adds, "She's gonna need that money when she realizes she never had a childhood."

It's not even dark yet, but I'm exhausted, so I hug my mom and start down the basement stairs for bed. I stop to look at the photographs that cover both sides of the walls. I space off, staring at them for about ten minutes. Baby pictures, sports, birthdays, vacations, family reunions, anniversaries, grandparents, aunts, uncles, and cousins, all the pictures are filled with smiling faces and captured laughter.

After a while my mom throws a dish towel down at me and says, "Focus, please. You were going to bed."

"Yeah, have these pictures always been here?"

She laughs. "I change them every once in a while, but yeah, we've always had family pictures on these stairs."

She walks back toward the kitchen, and I say "Huh" to no one. I must've run up and down these steps a million times, but never stopped to look at the pictures. I swear I've never seen this one of my grandma. She's about my age, and she's riding one of those Budweiser horses. The picture's got a few years of dust on it, so it must have been here a while. The frames are different sizes and only a couple of them match, but they're laid out carefully and spaced just right. What a pain in the ass it must have been to hang them. Not to mention, live the lives.

I'm looking at my parents' wedding picture when I hear my sister tell someone, "No, he's still on the stairs, zoning out."

Dad snaps me out of it and asks, "You need a ride to the set tomorrow?"

I tell him, "I'm good."

He asks, "Are you?"

I don't think he's talking about giving me a ride anymore. "Yeah. Sorry if I've been a dick lately."

He smiles. "Yeah. We don't have to see eye to eye all the time." He motions to the pictures on the wall and says, "But just remember, whatever happens with this movie . . . we're always here for you. Okay?"

I nod and he walks back into the kitchen. My family is pretty great.

17. PIZZA MAGNATE?

The next day starts much too early, but I'm excited. I was too nervous to enjoy yesterday, but now that I'm a one-day veteran I should be cool.

I step into the makeup trailer and say hi to the ladies already working on Hilary. "Wow, you're here early," I say.

Hilary can't move her face because of the airbrush that's being used on her upper lip, so she just flips me the bird.

The makeup ladies laugh, like she just said the funniest thing ever, and I smile because she's making an effort to be a smart-ass. The mood is way better this morning, so I ask the ladies if they could use that airbrush tool to touch up my bruises instead of the painful sponges and pencils.

They flatly say, "No."

I nod and wait my turn in the extra makeup chair. A new *US Weekly* is sitting on the counter, so I kick back, like I'm at the barbershop with my dad. I cross my right leg over my left because I've been thinking lately that I should try to be the kind of guy who crosses his legs from time to time. C. B. and Phil always stick one leg over the other one when they sit, and it looks pretty smart. I feel a little dumb when I do it, but I bet I look cool, so I keep it there. I look down at my ratty old Nikes and think back to when they were new, when I was going to a party at Maria's house last year to meet up with Abby for the first time. The grass stains weren't there, the soles weren't burned off at the edges, and I was pretty innocent. I had my first real kiss in these. My mom had no idea when she was paying for these suckers that I'd be getting action and shooting a movie in them someday.

I'm ripped out of my daydream when I finally focus on the cover of this *US Weekly*. My whole body flexes and my stomach sinks as I begin to process what I'm looking at. I squeal, "Haaaaaa!!!" when I realize I'm staring at myself! A blown-up grainy photograph of Hilary Idaho in bikini bottoms and Yours Truly with both of my hands out-stretched . . . smothering Hilary's hooters. We're standing on the bank of Grey Goose Lake, the rope swing is just out of frame, and her head is tilted back in laughter under the headline, "Sex on the Beach!"

I frantically flip to the article and yell, "Has anyone seen this *US Weekly*?"

A makeup girl says, "No, they just dropped it off."

Oh, I'm in big trouble. The next page contains fifteen different shots of me and Hilary totally looking like we're getting it on. Some of them are pretty hot, but all of them are lies! The first shot takes up the whole page. I'm lying on top of her in the mud; the caption reads, "Hilary Gets Dirty With Starvados!" *What the hell is a "Starvados"?* The next one shows me standing behind her with my hands on her hips, giving her a boost so that she can grab the rope swing a little higher. She's bent over, just slightly, her eyes are half closed, and her mouth is somewhat open. I know she's grunting with effort so she can reach that top notch, but that's *not* what it looks like! I'm flexed because

I'm lifting her, and I have to say, I look pretty buff.

This is outrageous! My mom is going to be mortified! I'm going to get fired! I'm going to be an absolute legend at school! And it's a complete lie. I flip the page and it's more of the same with smaller pictures and an image of the planet Earth with pinpoints sticking in it showing where the shots were supposedly taken. The caption asks, "Who is Hilary's new jet-setter?" with a shot of us running through the lobby of the President Hotel. The picture is next to California, and the caption reads, "Château Marmont, Los Angeles." We're holding hands and shielding our eyes, but we are nowhere near Los Angeles. And what the hell is a "chatêau"? Then they have a photo of us swimming at Grey Goose. It's connected to Italy and says, "Lake Como." What? Another one is in the Hy-Vee parking lot. We're getting out of the Escalade on Merrian Lane, but the line points to Florida and reads, "Rendezvous in South Beach!" When did they plant palm trees in front of the Hy-Vee? The bottom of the page says, "Meet Boy Toy . . ."

I flip the page so hard it rips out of the magazine. The next photo is just me, by myself, leaning on my bike, drinking a Mountain Dew, like a stone-cold pimp. It reads, "Pizza Magnate, Starvados Sbarro!!!" What the hell? It continues, "Grandson of Gennaro and Carmella Sbarro . . . heir to the Italian restaurant fortune," followed by a shot of me riding EJ's bike with Hilary on the pegs. The lies continue. "Sbarro placed third at the X Games, but he's Hilary's gold-medal man!"

Hey, *US Weekly* dickheads: As long as you're making stuff up, why did I have to get third place? And I remember leaning on my bike the other day, drinking a COKE, not

Mountain Dew! You can see that it's totally added in. My pinky finger is gone.

Sport Coat Phil flings the door to the trailer open and steps into the room like the Terminator. He's wearing his headset, sunglasses, and a scowl. He's got the *US Weekly* in his hand and is looking right at me when he snaps, "You got somethin' you want to tell me?!"

"Dude! I was just coverin' her—"

He interrupts. "I want an explanation, bitch, and if I find out you're lying, you're fired!"

"Dude! Okay, I was feeling them a little, but—"

He holds up his finger for me to shut up, adjusts his headset, and yells, "Get your fat ass over to the makeup trailer!"

I stand and say, "Uncalled for!" Then I stop and ask, "Aren't we in the makeup trailer?"

Hilary laughs and points to the blinking device in his ear before she says, "Carter, he's on the phone. Matilda authorized those photos . . . supposedly to create buzz about you before the movie comes out."

Matilda enters the trailer, and I guess Hilary's all made up and it's my turn, because a makeup lady starts poking at my face. Matilda explains that she made a deal with *People* magazine and they weren't supposed to run the photos for six months, but *US Weekly* intercepted them and ran the story they thought would sell the most magazines.

"And Mountain Dew," I add.

C. B. storms into the trailer like a tornado and yells, "Carter!"

I jump up and ask, "What the hell did *I* do?" mostly to get the makeup lady off me.

He holds up a copy of *US Weekly,* and I say, "Oh, yeah, that."

C. B. notices Phil and Matilda cowering in the corner. He throws the magazine at them. No one is saying anything, and the makeup lady is coming at me with her mascara stick, so I swat it away and ask, "Yo, what's a pizza magnet?"

He probably doesn't know either, because he yells, "I can't believe you're resorting to this kind of publicity already! We just started shooting!"

Phil barks, "We didn't mean for it to come out this early, but this is the game, C. B.! You're the one who cast a *nobody*! We'll need to make him a celebrity sooner or later."

C. B. throws up his hands and yells, "Starvados freakin' Sbarro?! This is going to be a great movie; we don't need this!"

The lady tilts my head back and starts pushing the sponge into my swollen chin like I called her ugly. "Owwww!"

Phil says to me, "Shut it, kid!" and then barks at C. B., "*This* is the difference between making twenty million and a hundred and twenty. It's unfortunate that they got his name wrong, but we can always change Carter's name."

"Huh?! Ouch!" I whine as I instinctively knock the sponge out of her hand and then apologize for doing it.

C. B. asks Phil if they can really do that, and Phil explains, "We make movies . . . we can do anything." He didn't bust out an evil cackling laugh afterward, but if this was my movie and I was the writer/director, he would have.

The makeup lady dabs goop onto one of my cuts until I jump out of the chair and pant, "Okay, I think I'm done!"

C. B. looks at Hilary and then at the makeup lady,

who's scowling at me. He says, "Okay, Starvados . . . let's get started."

I'm in a karate stance, looking at the makeup lady, when I ask, "Are you really gonna change my name?"

C. B. just laughs and steps out into the sunlight. The lady comes at me with a powder brush, so I draw my hands back and slowly back out of the trailer.

As if I didn't have enough crap to deal with . . . the first pair of eyes I connect with are attached to my angry ex-girlfriend. Abby's all lit up and doing her job as a stand-in, but her arms are crossed, and she's giving me a nasty look. A look that suggests she's seen the magazine, and even though she doesn't know the whole story, I have been tried and found guilty of something. Man, I can't deal with this right now, but I know that when I do, "innocence" is going to be a tough sell. I've got to get into character.

We shoot all the scenes inside the house, and they actually go great. Hilary and I are having fun, and it shows. C. B. even smiles a few times. The crew is joking around, calling me Starvados. I don't mind until Sport Coat Phil uses the nickname. The day flies by, like a proper summer day should, and C. B. yells, "That's a wrap, people!" before I know it.

I hurriedly change clothes and try to catch Abby before she breaks out, but Phil lets himself into my trailer to go over the next week's schedule. He explains that I've got two days off because Hilary is shooting the scenes I'm not in. I'm thinking about going to the pool and hanging out with my boys when Phil asks me if I'll volunteer to come to hang out with Hilary on set so that she stays on point and in a good mood. He thinks I'm a good influence. (Just so you know, you don't get paid for your "influence," and you're not allowed to tell the actor's union.) He looks at his clipboard and explains that my next day of actual work is at the train station, on Saturday. I have to be there at six a.m. to shoot action scenes. I'll be jumping onto a moving train and jumping off of it. They're also going to film me in the boxcar eating trash and reading books and writing in my journal.

I try to joke with Phil. "Wait a minute. Nobody told me I was going to have to read and write! I'm calling my agent!"

He doesn't laugh. I suspect he's not programmed for laughter, and that his earpiece is actually a neurotransmitter blinking his coordinates to the Hollywood mother ship. He's walking away, probably to go plug himself in for the night, when I ask, "Am I gonna have a stunt double or something when I jump from the train?"

He shatters my theory by laughing his ass off. I guess "nobodies" do their own stunts, and it's really funny when they think that they're "somebodies."

Abby is long gone and Hilary stops me before I can chase her down. She demands to know where I'm going and won't let me leave until I promise to come over to the President Hotel and do a yoga class and watch TV with her later tonight.

I ride over to Abby's house to explain the photos, but I couldn't get past the front door. Her mom/bouncer has obviously seen the US Weekly, because she greets me with a snarky, "Hello, Starvados!" and tells me to get lost. She says, "If Abby wants to talk, she'll call you," and then slams the knocker in my face.

When I walk into my own house, the phone starts ringing. Abby and I are so connected it's ridiculous! I let it ring three times so I don't seem too anxious, and then say, "Hey you . . ." all smooth.

She's just breathing heavily into the phone because she doesn't know what to say. I lower my voice and tell her, "It's okay, boo . . . I'm glad you called."

Then my ear fills with a dude's voice, "HUH!?"

Crap, it's just EJ. I recognize his panting. "Huuuu, uhhhh . . . dude . . . huuuu, uhhhh, I'm at Hy-Vee, huuuu, uhhhh . . . I think I'm freakin' out!"

"Is there a special on tenderloins, you sick freak?"

"Huhhhh, uhhh . . . No . . . I'm at the checkout . . . huuu, uhhhh, I'm lookin' at . . . uh, *US Weekly*."

"Oh yeeaaah, you like that, don't you?!"

He gasps, "Dude, are you an international playboy? And you didn't tell me? Huuu, uhhhh . . . Who are you, man?!" he demands.

"Come on—"

"Is your name Will Carter?! Answer me!"

"Dude, we've hung out every day since kindergarten. . . . How could I be a pizza magnate?"

"What the hell *is* a pizza magnet?" he asks.

"I think my mom has one on the fridge."

He tries to ask about the movie, but I tell him I have to go.

He barks, "Wait a friggin' minute! I haven't heard from you in weeks, and if you're doinkin' Hilary Idaho, I need to know about it!"

My immediate reaction is to tell him that I absolutely . . . *am*! That we "doinked" in all those spots they have pictures of, and twenty others that they didn't catch, but I know it's wrong to lie and rub that fib in my best friend's face—a guy who'd never lie to me . . . but who *would* tell me every detail, sound, smell, and position from every damn sexual experience he's ever had, with three different girls, when he knows I've never had it! So I coldly reply, "Dude, I'm not tryin' to kiss and tell."

EJ squeals with excitement from this inferred confirmation. "You hit that all over town! You smacked that ass, didn't you?" I hear the sound of magazine pages flipping underneath his giggling. I know he's miming the smacking of an ass as he shouts, "Whoooah! Yeah, she's ridin' the baloney pony express—"

A cracking sound causes me to remove the phone from my ear, and I can vaguely hear his mom yelling, "Emilio . . . potty mouth . . . bad boy!" The line goes dead, and I laugh for ten minutes at the thought of EJ standing in the Hy-Vee checkout line, holding up an *US Weekly* and humping the air while yelling, "Smack that ass!" and "Baloney pony express!" I guarantee you, that cracking sound was the cell phone hitting the floor after his mom tackled him into the candy rack before dragging him out to the car like a mischievous toddler (not a guy who was six foot three, last time we measured).

18. GET TO THE PAIN

The next week flies by, and everything is going pretty well, except for the massive bruise on my hip and the constant throbbing in my left shoulder. (Just so you know, when you jump from a train that's going twenty miles an hour, remember that the earth is not moving with you, and when someone tells you to, "Hit the ground running!" they're not trying to inspire you with general, clever, old-timey advice. Rather, they are giving you specific directions as to what to do with your feet when you jump from a moving locomotive.) And while there are a lot of disadvantages to hiring a "nobody" to star in your movie, you will save a lot of money on stuntmen, and the union only seems to care if the "somebodies" are in danger. According to Phil, I rock!

Sometimes we get the scenes right away and only shoot a couple of takes, and other times C. B. will make us do them over and over until Phil reminds him of that "one minute on a film set costs a thousand dollars" rule, and we move on to the next one. I like the acting a lot, but I officially love this movie-set thing called the "craft service table." It's a free snack bar that stocks everything from M&M's to vitamin-infused popcorn. It's all you can eat, all day, and they never run out of stuff, and they don't yell at you for eating too much. I guarantee this is the reason Marlon Brando got so fat.

Hilary's breath hasn't smelled like booze since the first day, but her behavior can be a little bit hit-or-miss. Sometimes she's super sweet and polite to everyone, and other times she's a freak-a-zoid bitch. I know from experience that chicks can flip out for no reason, but Hilary can get so pissed so quickly it makes everyone a little bit nervous. Once, a lady brought her a cold water, and she threw it at her because she likes "ROOM TEMPERATURE, BITCH!!!" and everyone should know these details after weeks of shooting. I think what she wants is for people to be honest with her and not treat her special, but she doesn't know how to say it. I've definitely figured out how to make her laugh: you just make fun of her. She loves it! I make fun of her orange skin and how little she eats. Even though her boobs are real, I still put a couple grapefruits from the craft service table under my T-shirt and ask, "Do these look natural?" I goof on *The Get Up Gang* and do impressions of their rap songs, and I do a two-minute version of *Cheer! The Musical* that I still think is too long. I sing, "Go! Fight! Weeeeiiiiieeeyaaaaahhheeeiiiiyaaaahhhhna!" all the time, and she dies laughing.

C. B. added a few new scenes, but we've finally finished all of the interior shots at Saur mansion. We're getting ready to shoot the kissing/crying scene at the end of the movie, and we're both diarrhea-nervous about it. We've rehearsed it so many times, but C. B. still wants us to "keep it natural." We've improv'd the scene fifty different ways. . . . The only way we could make it different is if we tried to do it in Spanish. I'm not scared to kiss Hilary anymore, but I feel like a robot when I try to cry. I've been daydreaming about funerals and watching depressing movies. I'm trying to think of every sad thing that's ever happened to me, but nothing is working! I am incredibly depressed but not producing any tears.

The camera and lights are all set up for the scene. We usually walk through the blocking and say the lines a few times before we shoot. I know this crap like I know my own name, but Hilary keeps taking these big dramatic pauses before saying her lines. She's scrunching up her face and breathing really heavily. I'm not really concentrating on my work because I'm trying to figure out what the hell she's doing. We get to the part where she's supposed to get emotional, and she busts out wailing, "HUUUUAAAAHHHHH!!!" Her character is supposed to be upset that this relationship is breaking up, but she's acting like her village was just bombed. Tears are shooting out of her eyes. I'm supposed to be torn up as well, but I'm just watching the Hilary Idaho show. The cameras aren't even rolling, but C. B. yells, "CUT!!!" as if they are. He springs up from his chair and runs over to us. He grabs her elbow and barks, "What are you doing?!"

Hilary looks really shocked that he stopped her brilliant performance, and explains, "I'm just trying something."

C. B. is usually pretty careful around Hilary. He knows that she's fragile, so he keeps his comments pretty positive for the most part, but this hysterical crying has set him off. "How about you *try* the stuff we've been working on during rehearsal, and feel the emotion of the scene? How about you *try* to be honest, and not manufacture this BS crying? And while you're at it, *try* not to ruin my film!"

Tears well up in Hilary's eyes (real ones), and I think I know what C. B. is trying to do. He's trying to break her down, to get her to feel more vulnerable. He's hoping it will spill over into the lines like it did for me and Abby at the audition, but he may have gone too far because Hilary is not looking sad so much as really pissed off.

C. B. stomps back to the camera and yells to the crew that we're going to try to shoot one. My heart jumps into my throat, but I'm still worried about Hilary, so I ask, "Are you okay?"

If her frustration was looking for an outlet . . . it finds me. She yells, "Don't talk to me! You think I don't know what he's doing? I'm a professional; I can get myself where I need to be."

She yells to Phil that she's taking a break and storms off toward her trailer. Phil shoots C. B. a mean look and follows her into the RV.

I guess I'm relieved that the crying scene had to be postponed, but I'm pretty concerned about Hilary. Phil eventually exits her trailer, and she locks the door behind him. She refuses to come out, so we break for lunch early. I'm still focused on the upcoming scene until Matilda pulls the Escalade up to Hilary's door and they drive away really fast. Phil's assistant tells me that she was just going back to the hotel for a nap and she would be right back, but C. B. looks really worried. After two hours she still hasn't returned, so we stop for the day. What a relief! I guess we'll get back to the crying scene after we've filmed the stuff at my school. At first I was stoked to be getting off early, but the more I think about her "nap," the more anxious I become.

Since I'm done for the day, I ride to the pool and say hi to my boys. I lock up at the bike racks and give a nod to the front-desk girl before ducking into the locker room. Her jaw dropped when she looked up from her copy of *US Weekly*. Could it be? Oh yeah, Starvados freakin' Sbarro is standing before you! She didn't have a chance to ask for my autograph or check to see my season pass as I blew past. You can smell the sunscreen and hear the shouting and laughter before you even get to the pool area. A smile rips across my face when I see my boys jumping off the diving boards. Man, I've really missed this place. Daniel Day-Lewis may stay in character for the whole shooting process, but I think I need to take some breaks.

Nutt is just doing a gainer off the high dive when I walk up. EJ, Bag, and Doc are wearing their official red life-guard trunks. I know that I'm a movie star now, but I'm still totally jealous that they are getting paid to hang out at the pool. J-Low, Hormone, and Nutt are just hanging out . . . not getting paid.

Bag spots me first and yells, "Look who finally showed up," and punches me in the shoulder (ouch).

EJ slaps me in the neck (ouch) and asks, "Where the hell have you been?"

They gather around me, but these fools know exactly where I've been. "Don't you guys read *US Weekly*? I've been in Miami, L.A., Europe . . . I'm a jet-setter now."

Everyone is chuckling, except Nutt. He doesn't usually get sarcasm, so he asks, "How the hell did you get to Italy?"

EJ replies, "He teleported, dumbass."

I add, "They made all that stuff up for the magazine."

Bag sniffs my T-shirt and inquires, "Carter, why do you smell like a petting zoo?"

"My character doesn't have a shower, so I'm not

bathing very much right now. Yo, who's got some trunks I can borrow?"

EJ gives the other guys a mischievous look that I don't like. He slyly says, "You don't need trunks, dog . . . You need a bath!"

A hand clamps down on my shoulder, and I try to spin away before they can get a hold of me. Dang it. I yell "Don't!" as I push Doc off me. Hormone and Bag grab my ankles as Nutt and EJ secure my arms. I flex down and try to squirm away, but they hoist me off the ground like a rag doll. Damn, they're getting stronger.

I'm flailing pretty good as Bag yells, "There's a bathtub right here!"

I try to plead with them. "No, I'm still in my costume!"

But there is no reasoning with a group of dudes when they're planning to punk you. I'm moving fast as they laugh and drive their legs toward the water. I try to say, "Please!!! The costume designer will kill me if—"

SPLASH!!! EJ, Bag, Nutt, Doc, J-Low, Hormone, me and my custom-fitted vintage wardrobe crash into the cold water. It actually feels really good, but I can't stop to enjoy it. My boys are all howling with laughter as I swim to the edge and try to haul my soggy, fully clothed ass out of the pool. "You guys suck! I'm gonna get bitched at so bad for this!" They are still giggling in the pool and splashing me. "You don't get it, this isn't funny, I could get fired for this! A team of people made these clothes for me!"

I storm off toward the front gates, but EJ hops out of the pool and chases me down. "Yo, wait! I'm sorry, man. We didn't know that was a costume. You dress like that every day."

"I *said* I was wearing a costume!"

He replies, "Yeah, but we already had you off the ground by then. And you do kind of stink."

I throw up my hands and say, "I'm trying to stay in character. I'm trying to do something here, and you have no idea how much pressure I'm under."

EJ stops walking and asks, "How are we supposed to know that? We haven't seen you all summer."

I just keep going into the locker room and say, "Whatever!" The sound echoes off the concrete walls as I blow past the front-desk girl and jump on my bike.

I throw the clothes in the dryer at home and hope for the best. When I put them back on, they're a bit tighter, but hopefully if I move around in them, the costume department won't notice that they're less smelly.

That night, I cruise over to the President Hotel to see how Hilary is doing. I wave to the paparazzi guys and head up to the penthouse. Matilda is waiting for me when the elevator doors pop open.

"WHOA!" I scream. "I mean, hello. S'up?"

She's nervously pacing around the living room and tells me that Hilary is still asleep. Matilda seems stressed like I've never seen her before. I was right: she really cares about the body she's guarding.

I ask, "Is everything okay?"

Tears are welling up in her eyes as she stares at me. "No, it's not. Hilary took a bunch of pills today in her trailer."

I don't say anything, because I'm not sure what she means. Matilda continues, "She overdosed," as she reaches into her pocket and hands me a bag of pills. "Do you recognize any of these?"

The letters printed on one of them look familiar, *CIBA 16.* My eyes light up, "Yeah, this is ADHD medicine; my boy EJ takes these."

She picks them out of my palm and asks, "Did you give them to her?"

"No."

She sighs, "I didn't think so . . ." and I start to say thanks, but then she continues, "I know you have ADD, but if you took the medication, you wouldn't be such a space cadet." (Bitch.) "Where can I find this EJ?"

"No way. I like Hilary, but I'm not letting you take out my best friend. We may not be rich, but we aren't drug dealers."

She doesn't get to respond because Hilary yells from the bedroom, "Matilda, open this door, you bitch!"

She walks over and unlocks the latch. Hilary springs from the dark room and has to adjust to the lights before she screeches, "How the hell did I get back here?"

Matilda is so mad, she doesn't say anything, so I tell her, "You took too many goofballs, Marilyn. You passed out."

Her head drops and she starts crying. "Damn it! Who knows?"

Matilda tells her, "Just Carter."

Hilary smears her mascara and smiles at me. "Good. You won't tell anyone, will you?"

She looks sad and as fragile as a porcelain doll. Like I could push her over and she would shatter into a million pieces. She's rubbing her bloodshot eyes with one hand and gripping the sofa with the other.

She explains, "I didn't mean to do it, Carter."

What the hell am I supposed to do with this? If I tell

Phil, won't he just blow it off? Or would he call her mom and shut the movie down? Her mom would be pissed, but probably tell Matilda to handle it. We're so close to finishing the film that even C. B. wouldn't do anything that might jeopardize his movie. He's really nice to her, but I think he'd be fine if she jumped off a cliff after he got the last shot. The best thing I could do for Hilary is call *US Weekly* and lay it all out. Public shame has kept more than a few people on the straight and narrow, but it would definitely end the filming and crush her. I reluctantly smile and say, "No, I won't . . . if you promise you won't do any more."

She smiles like a great weight has been lifted off her, but then she gets pissed, quick. "This is your first movie, you little shit! And it'll be your last if you do the wrong thing here. Who do you think you are? You think we're friends? Do you have any idea how lucky you are to even be in the same room with me? You don't give me demands or conditions. I'm Hilary Idaho, bitch!"

Wow, my chest hurts like she just kicked it. I would have preferred a punch in the face to that. She motions for the elevator and tells Matilda, "Get him out of here. And take a shower, boy. You stink. Idiot thinks he's Marlon Brando!"

The doors close, and I'm able to push the button for the lobby before I start crying. I just stopped by to say hello, not to have my faith in humanity challenged. I have no idea who the hell I am anymore. I've been pretending to be someone else so much that I seem to have lost myself. I need to talk to somebody about this, or I'm going to explode. But I've been so busy turning everyone in my life away that I have no idea who to turn to. I walk out into the lobby and wipe the snot from my nose as a photographer flashes his camera in my face and asks, "Trouble in paradise, Starvados?"

I don't answer him because it won't make any difference. I'll just wait for next week's tabloids to find out why Starvados Sbarro was crying at Château Marmont.

I feel so alone as I pedal toward home. I could talk to Lynn, except she's working like a dog for the costume designer's assistant, and she doesn't have time to deal with my issues. My parents would freak out and not let me be in the movie. I dialed Abby's number about ten times, but I never let it go through. I really thought that she might call me . . . like she can sense how much I need her, but she didn't, so I keep it zipped like Hilary thought I would.

We get back into the shooting, and she acts like nothing happened. We're mostly doing walking shots on the streets of Merrian. Hilary is trying to be really nice to me and the rest of the crew, but I can't help but stiffen up when she gets close. I'm like a dog that's been smacked one too many times, and I can't help but flinch. People take pictures and stop to gawk, even if Hilary isn't in the shot. I guess the thinking is, if you're important enough to have this crew running around, and the camera is pointing at you . . . you must be a somebody! It's pretty cool because I know (along with the rest of the cast and crew) that I'm a nobody, but the general public has no idea! Feel free to worship me, people.

We're almost two weeks behind schedule, and Phil is running around like a chicken with its head cut off. He's yelling at everyone to do their jobs faster, but his hysterics seem to have the opposite effect on people. When someone is doing their best and someone yells at them to "HURRY

THE HELL UP!!!" it seems to fluster them and actually slow things down. It sure as hell isn't my problem; I can't act any faster, but Phil still waits for me outside the bathroom as if the whole production is waiting for me to poop. This dude's going to give me hemorrhoids!

As much as I've been dreading the crying scene, I've been looking forward to shooting the scenes at Merrian High. It's cool to be at school when there aren't so many people, and the ones that are here are staring at me like I'm a big shot. A couple of cute girls are checking me out when I stumble out of the makeup trailer. I walk over to the craft service table and eat M&M's until one of the girls says hi to me.

"Hey," I mumble with a mouth full of chocolate.

They ask if I'll sign their copies of *US Weekly*.

"Sure, d-d-do you guys go to college around here?" I ask, knowing they're in high school . . . because I'm so smooth! I'm thinking about inviting them back to my trailer when they look down at my scribble and ask, "Who the hell is *Carter*?"

I shrug as if to say, "Who do you think, baby?"

They walk away in disgust, and I hear the tall one say, "I thought that was Starvados Sbarro."

The short one adds, "No, that boy is obviously his stand-in. He's no pizza magnate. . . . You can tell."

I ask the empty bowl of M&M's, "Please tell me what a pizza magnet is."

We're still waiting for Hilary to arrive, and Phil seems especially pissed off today. His assistant tells me that they're setting up a classroom shot, and they're going to try to add Hilary's face to someone else's body in postproduction.

"You can do that?" I ask.

He seems annoyed when he says, "We make movies . . . *We* can do anything."

He's an assistant, so all *he* can really *do* is get coffee, but whatever.

McDougle is playing the teacher who rats me out after inspiring me to write a great paper about my terrible life. She has all the dialogue, and probably needs to concentrate, but I see her coming out of her RV, so I go over and say hi.

In a *Kung Fu* accent I mutter, "De masta and de student finaaally meet on de field of baddalle!"

She replies, "Carter, how much candy have you eaten today?"

"De Masta say, nooo too much can-dy for de powaful stu-dent! Whuuuuu-aaaaaahhh—!"

She interrupts my crane kick. "Carter!"

"Yeah?"

"Stay focused," she demands.

We walk into the classroom full of extras. Abby is sitting with Jeremy, so I give them a nod and take my seat behind them. Jeremy waves, but Abby doesn't seem to notice. She's wearing one of Hilary's costumes, and she has blue dots glued all over her face. C. B. is intensely working out how he wants the camera to move, and another guy is using the tape measure to figure out how far away Abby's dots are from the lens. I should be focusing on this scene. I don't have any lines; I'm just supposed to look anxious and angry, but I'm trying, unsuccessfully, to get Abby to look at me. *HELLO!!! The star of the movie is over here! The guy that the camera and lights are pointing at?! The guy who doesn't have dots all over his face so he can be edited out later?* I flex my jaw just in case she looks over. I clear my throat. Why the hell won't she look at me?

C. B. yells "Cut" before I realize we were shooting anything, and he seems really happy. "Nice work, Carter . . . that was some raw emotion," he says as he checks the gate and starts breaking down the camera.

Phil tells everyone that Hilary is finally here, so we're moving on to the hallway scenes.

Abby is told to change clothes and remove the dots from her face because she's going to have to be an extra for the rest of the day. She and Jeremy are in the hall shot with a few other kids, and so is College Carter Dumbass. Great! I was told he got the part of Jeff Becker, the d-bag that tries to steal my girl in the movie. Abby would say, "Art imitates life," if she was talking to me.

C. B. directs Abby and Jeremy to walk through the frame holding hands like they're boyfriend-girlfriend. I think it's pretty funny, but Abby is all business, so while they're rehearsing I mumble, "Cute couple."

Abby mouths the word, "Concentrate!" very seriously in response . . . as if I need her help here. Like, who the hell does that little extra think she is?! Telling *me*, the pretty-much star of this movie, what to do with my—

"Carter!" C. B. yells in my face and snaps his fingers. "Are you ready to shoot one?"

I look toward Abby and say, "Shoooot, I was born ready."

She rolls her eyes, and C. B. walks back to his camera.

This is the scene where Hilary tells me that Jeff Becker has asked her to go to prom. She talks about it as a joke, like "ha-ha," but my character knows that she'd really like to go,

179

and gets pissed about it. I have this whole monologue I'm supposed to say, but I forgot to look at it during our last break. Hilary must be having one of her bad days because she doesn't even say hello to me when they usher her onto the set. We walk through the moves a few times to get the background people to move correctly (friggin' extras!). C. B. asks Jeremy to stop "prancing" a few times, but Jeremy is too fabulous for his own good, so C. B. recasts College Carter Dumbass to play Abby's fake boyfriend.

I quietly tell C. B., "Yo, that's the guy playing Jeff Becker . . . would he really be walking down the hall holding hands with this other girl?"

C. B. explains, "They're background; it'll just look like shapes walking through the frame."

"Oh yeah, cool, um, couldn't you get one of these other extras to do that? I don't care; it's just that that guy's nineteen and she's fifteen, so it may be illegal, you know?"

C. B. glares at me and says, "How about *I* direct *this* movie and you get the next one?"

"Yeah, cool, whatever—"

He barks, "Background action!"

The extras start to move, and Abby whispers something into College Carter Dumbass's ear. He giggles and whispers something in response.

C. B. yells, "Hilary and Carter . . . ACTION!"

I'm just supposed to be getting stuff out of my locker at this point, so I lean against the wall to try and pull myself together and not freak out. Did Abby just make fun of me to him again? Hilary walks up and says her line about the dude asking her out. I'm supposed say, "'Why don't you just go to the dance?'" but I'm so pissed off at Abby while

I'm listening to Hilary that I just bite my lip and shake my head.

Hilary says her line, " 'Isn't that lame?' " and I'm not getting it together, at all! I'm shaking with anger. I still haven't said a word, and I don't think I'll come up with anything anytime soon. My brain is so defective and filled with Abby's little mind games that I decide to head-butt the locker, hard. *BANG!!!*

Hilary stops acting and asks, "What's wrong with you?" I look her in the eyes and try not to fall down. I grab my head and struggle to remember why the hell I just head-butted a locker. Hilary has no idea that I'm ridiculously pissed off at a couple of whispering extras. I rock back on my heels, and she grabs my wrist to steady me before asking, "Why are you doing this?" But I jerk my hand away. She gets back into character and decides to skip over my monologue about why I hate prom. She tries to say her next line, " 'I was joking . . . I don't even want to—' "

BANG!!! I kick the locker as hard as I can. The metal crunches under my foot. Hilary jumps back in shock and repeats her last line, " 'I was joking!' " but I don't even acknowledge her; I just glance toward Abby and limp out of frame.

C. B. yells, "CUT!"

Phil and his assistant ask, "What the hell was that?"

It's dead quiet until C. B. exclaims, "*That* was amazing!" and starts clapping. Then everyone is applauding my screwup . . . except for Abby, Hilary, and the crew guy who's going to have to replace the locker door. C. B. continues, "Carter you really are the next Daniel Day-Lewis! Cut the fluff and get to the pain, brother!"

I nod a half-assed thank-you and hobble toward craft service to get some ice for my swelling head and foot. I need to figure out what scene is coming up next, and why I'm such a freak.

19. J-J-JEREMY AND THE JETS

I change my shirt and look over the script as the knot on my head continues to grow. It's a big fight scene that takes place in the middle of the movie. It begins with Hilary/ Maggie exiting the school with a group of jocks, and they discover me digging in the Dumpster. The guys call me a bunch of names and then beat me up. This event definitely happened to C. B., because he's talked a lot about it, and it seems like he's really looking forward to reliving the moment. I guess putting a humiliating experience from your life into a movie, book, or play would be therapeutic and possibly the ultimate revenge. It's kind of sad, though, because I know a-holes like the guys who beat him up. The jerks who think it's funny to pick on someone weaker so they can feel stronger. I won't mention it to C. B., but I bet those kids don't even remember punching him or calling him a dirtbag or throwing him into a trash can. I'll bet they recall the time they gave a homeless guy a dollar or helped an old lady cross the street. They may have even read *Down Gets Out*, or they'll see the movie and have no idea their cruelty has not been forgotten. It's brewed inside a guy for fifteen years. A guy who now drives a Ferrari. So whatever, I guess.

Phil's assistant walks me to a ladder that's set up in the

trash area behind the school. I've never been back here and I know why . . . It stinks, bad! You wouldn't think it would smell this bad in the summer. And you might think that for a movie they'd bring in a special Dumpster for the actors, a new Dumpster, perhaps a *clean* Dumpster, or a Dumpster without maggots! You'd be wrong. The lights are all set up and everyone is watching me. I had such a good response to my last couple of scenes that I don't want to ruin it by puking all over myself, so I hold it down, get into character, and try not to breathe through my nose as I climb into the disgusting metal box. Trash is all over the place, but they've got one of the bags marked for me to pull food out of. It's got plastic pizza and something that looks like meat loaf inside. It may be a prop, but it smells like poop.

C. B. holds the camera over the edge and films me stuffing an old backpack with this weird cuisine. I try not to look too disgusted as I do it. C. B. rotates the camera back to shoot me climbing out and my reaction to being discovered by the group of kids. Hilary is supposed to be in the middle of the gang, and she's supposed to look embarrassed for me and then run away. But when I pop my head over the side of the Dumpster, I see Abby and Jeremy standing there with a group of extras. A smile flashes across my mouth before I can get a hold of it. I shake my head in disgust for ruining the shot, and climb the rest of the way out. Abby screwed me up again!

C. B. says "Cut," then looks up from his camera and asks, "What was with the smile?"

"Sorry, I was expecting Hilary, and when I saw somebody else it jacked me up."

C. B. explains, "Yeah, she needed to take another break,

so we had to use your girlfriend as a stand-in—"

"Ex-girlfriend," I clarify.

"Uh-huh."

I whisper, "Abby's not my girlfriend—"

He continues, "Whatever, Carter, what you just did was brilliant. . . . For your character to look up, into the most embarrassing situation of his life and see the girl that he's hopelessly in love with, and smile just before the humiliation sets in. That's genius—"

"I am not hopelessly in love with her."

C. B. grabs me by the shoulders and quietly says, "I'm talking about the movie. But you should know, for your own sake, that you are hopelessly in love with that girl."

I exhale pointedly as if to say, "Whatever."

C. B. tells the crew that we're moving on to the next shot, where the boys in the group heckle me and give me the beat-down. They will add Hilary into the scene when she's ready. The scene is quick, and I know the lines, but what C. B. hasn't gone over is how the other actors are going to *pretend* to kick my ass.

They have two cameras set up to capture the fight, but no one has gone over the choreography. The lights and sound equipment are all ready, but they've done a horrible job of casting this group of ass kickers. C. B. has been complaining about this problem for a while, but Phil always tells him, "When you produce your own films, you can fly in actors for the small parts and cast the locals in the leads. Until then, we're using the cheap local talent for these nothing characters."

So Jeremy, College Carter Dumbass, and a bunch of other drama-department types are playing tough guys. I don't know how this is going to work, but I climb into the Dumpster anyway.

He has them huddled up like a powder-puff football team. Dang it. He's trying to psych them up to beat me down, and I realize why no one has talked about the pretend stage fighting . . . because C. B. wants it "real." Yet another great thing about casting a "nobody" in your movie is that, not only does he not get to call his agent, union, or stage mother to stop you from putting him in a Dumpster with maggots or throw him from a moving train . . . but he also won't blow the whistle on your pill-popping starlet, and you can actually kick his ass when the script calls for it! How awesome am I?!

C. B. calls "Action," and College Carter Dumbass says his line with a slight British accent. " 'What do you think you are doing, dirtbag?' "

I'm just trying to climb out of the can, and I don't look at them when I say my line. " 'This isn't what it looks like, guys. I'm on the recycling committee—' "

Eventually I look up at this posse of pussies assembled to kick my ass, quite possibly the only crew less intimidating than the Get Up Gang. Jeremy is standing off to the side with his hands on his hips. His jaw is flexed and his head is tilted, like he's trying to be tough, but it's the gayest thing I've ever seen, so I start laughing.

C. B. angrily yells "Cut!" because a bunch of the crew guys are cracking up too, and now this band of merry men are really mad at me. Skinny arms are crossed, faces turn red, and I can't stop cackling.

"Sorry, everybody. My bad," I say.

C. B. approaches the *West Side Story* hooligans (Abby

made me watch it) and tries to hype them up again. He tells everyone to "Be professional!" before he calls "Action," and I start to climb out of the Dumpster. College Carter Dumbass says his line, louder this time, and I take a deep disgusting breath. I focus on the nasty smell, and it keeps me from laughing as I tell my shoes, "'I'm on the recycling committee.'" I shoulder my backpack and try to walk past. I hope it looks like I'm trying to focus on catching up to Maggie and not that I can't look at these emos without cracking up. But then Jeremy slaps my face, hard, and screeches, "'Look at us when we're talking to you, dirtbag!'"

I grab my face and ask, "Dude!?"

Before anyone can say anything else, College Carter Dumbass shoves me in this very theatrical way. It doesn't hurt, or move me, so I knock his arms away and push him back. He stumbles and then falls to the ground.

C. B. shakes his head. "Cut!"

I throw up my hands like, "What am I supposed to do?"

Phil yells at everyone to break for lunch. He and C. B. seem extra stressed. Phil is telling C. B. to make it work, and C. B. is yelling at Phil for ruining his film. I think they both really want to save the scene, so I walk up and regretfully say, "Hey, I know a few dudes who wouldn't mind kickin' my ass."

Phil asks how soon my boys could get here, and I tell him, "Depends on how much you're paying."

C. B. interjects, "Two hundred a piece, cash, for about an hour's work."

"They'll be here in ten minutes."

Phil looks pissed, but he knows how unbelievable the

fight would be if Jeremy and the Jets were allowed to continue.

Everyone goes into the school cafeteria to eat, but I'm not hungry after hanging out in that Dumpster. Phil gives me his cell phone, and I start to round up my boys.

20. POTENTIAL

Bag answers the phone, "Merrian Aquatic Center, this is Matthew, how can I help you?" He's on "phone detail" after he got removed from lifeguarding for flirting with a girl from Hooker High. It's not against the rules to flirt with Hookers, but he was supposed to be watching the baby pool at the time, and a kid almost drowned as he was asking the Hooker, "Is that bikini top felt?—do you want it to be?" EJ said that the toddler's mom grabbed the kid a few seconds after he went under and that there wasn't that much danger, but Bag got demoted anyway.

In my best deep adult voice I say, "Yeah, uh, this is Doctor Bill MeHoff . . . I'm tryin' to get in touch with my son, Jack."

Bag responds like the cocky prick he is. "Uh, huh . . . gimme the last name again, doc?"

I repeat the name and then I hear the phone hit the desk and the unmistakable crackle of an old loudspeaker. Bag announces to the pool and surrounding community, "Jack MeHoff, Jack MeHoff, you gotta phone call . . . Jack Me—Ahhh, son of a BITCH!"

"Bitch," echoes around the aquatic center a few times before he picks up the phone again and yells, "Who the hell is this?"

"I told ya, it's Doctor MeHoff . . . callin' to let you know that your sex change operation has been rescheduled—"

"Carter! You butt plug, I'm gonna get fired for yellin' *jack me off* over the loudspeaker!"

"Good 'cause I got you a better job. I need you to round up EJ and the boys to come up to school and kick my ass for twenty minutes. You'll get paid two hundred bucks each."

I hear the pool manager's voice boom in the background, "Get off that phone and get outta my aquatic center, now!"

Bag doesn't say anything to his former boss; he just tells me, "See you in a few," and the line clicks dead.

I'm just ending a call with Nick Brock when EJ, Nutt, Bag, Doc, J-Low, and Hormone screech into the parking lot in the CRX. I point to them like a pimp, and shoot Sport Coat Phil a nod. There's more than enough weight to hold the car down, but the tires are completely bald and it's going way too fast. It looks pretty cool, like a drift car skidding around the corner, until they hit a curb that sends the dudes in the hatchback into the air, shuffling them around. The CRX flies into the grass and busts a donut before the engine sputters and dies. Hormone pulls up the emergency brake, and they climb out as if they found the perfect parking spot.

"S'up?!" Nutt asks, slapping my hand.

Doc says, "Heard they're givin' out cash money to kick your ass, Carter."

EJ punches me in the shoulder before he says, "I'd kick your dirty ass for free, Starvados!" He gives me a nod that seems to say, "You are forgiven for yelling at us."

J-Low asks, "Daaang, are you wearin' Dumpster cologne?"

Bag slaps me in the neck really hard and says, "Jack

MeHoff, huh?! You son of a—"

The guys are all laughing as C. B. walks up clapping and yelling, "Hell yeah, that's what we're looking for! You guys are perfect!"

He only thinks my boys are tough because of the last guys he was working with. When Nick Brock's truck rumbles into the parking lot, C. B.'s reminded of how intimidating high school guys can be. Bart hops out of the passenger side, followed by the Skeleton, who flicks his lit cigarette into the back of Bart's neck. A spark flies into the air as the butt falls into his T-shirt. Bart jumps around and squeals, "OWWWWEEE!" until it drops out, and he turns to slap the Skeleton's face. The Skeleton puts Bart in a headlock before slamming his skull into the truck door. They roll around the parking lot until Nick yells, "Knock it off!" and they stroll over.

Phil looks relieved by how quickly my friends arrived, but slightly worried about the can of worms he may have opened. C. B. stops grinning and asks us, "Are you guys ready to give Carter a beat-down?"

He throws his tattooed arm around my neck before they can answer. He leads me toward the set, and the guys follow. As we approach the trash area, EJ shakes his head in disbelief at the trucks, RVs, crew guys, lights, and cameras. "Man, you're really *starring* in a movie?!"

I give him a nod and reply, "Not really, I just have a lot of lines."

C. B. turns around and says, "Yeah he is, and he's doing a great job. We need you guys to help us make this fight scene believable, and after you do that, you're going to shoot a quick scene with Hilary Idaho." The guys high-five each other, and Nutt starts humping the air. Matilda stands beside Hilary's trailer and glares at him.

C. B. continues, "You gotta ridicule and beat the hell out of Carter first!"

They nod their heads in unison as if that was the most normal request they've ever heard. I try to tell them that there's no reason to actually beat me up, but C. B. cuts me off and clarifies, "No, guys, this is real! This happened to me. . . . These assholes punched and kicked me until my nose broke and my ribs cracked, just because they could, and I want the audience to feel the pain that I felt. I want them to be furious with you for assaulting such a vulnerable character—"

Hormone raises his hand and asks, "What does 'vulnerable' mean?"

Bart translates. "Pussy."

They all nod.

C. B. continues. "Yes, if you're not savage enough, it doesn't work. You have to impact this character's life."

The Skeleton punches his palm and laughs. "We're gonna impact your face, Carter!"

C. B. cheers, "Yeah! Call him Chris or dirtbag, though, when we film. This is the turning point of this character's journey, when he decides that this town is poison and he has to leave."

My boys are getting pretty fired up about kicking my ass, and it's worrying me a little. I climb into the Dumpster, and they take their positions on the other side of the loading dock with College Carter Dumbass. C. B. has them huddled up, and it seems a lot more natural for these dudes than the last group. He's really up in their faces, and he keeps pointing toward me. My best friends are scowling at me and growing more aggressive with every glance. As if I'm their sworn enemy and they're finally getting the chance to take me out.

I ask C. B. if he wants to walk through one, but he just puts the camera over his shoulder and says, "No, let's shoot it and see what happens! Don't be afraid to be COMPLETE assholes!" He calls out, "Camera ready!" then points at the guys like an army sergeant and yells, "ACTION!"

I bend down and stuff a few more bits of meat loaf into my bag. I'm zipping it up when College Carter Dumbass yells his line (without the British accent). "'Hey, dirtbag! Whadaya think you're doin'?'"

It actually sounds like he means it this time. I peer over the edge and see J-Low and Doc give a couple of menacing cackles as they saunter over. Nutt pushes J-Low to the ground and jumps into the air with excitement before yelling, "S'up, you FAGGOT?!"

My boys all look at him. This is their first scene in a movie, but they're pretty sure Nutt just went too far. C. B. moves his eye away from the camera, shakes his head, and says, "Uhhh, cut. Okay, guys, go back to your first position, and let's try that again. Maybe dial down the asshole a little." He points at Nutt and says, "You . . . don't talk anymore."

Bart pushes his brother and says, "Yeah, dumbass," as if he hadn't taught his little brother to be grossly inappropriate since birth.

Phil yells, "Quiet on the set!"

And C. B. calls, "ACTION!"

I duck back down and make sure I have enough of this

plastic pizza in my bag. Uh, it reeks!

The other Carter yells the line again, and I look over the side; they are ready to rumble. Nutt has his hands stuffed into his pockets to help restrain his enthusiasm.

C. B. moves the camera with me as I climb down the side and say, " 'Hey guys, this isn't what it looks like. I-I-I'm on the recycling committee.' "

Hormone jumps in on the action and gives himself a line. "What recycling committee, you stutterin' little bitch?! I've never seen your dirty ass at the student council meetings!"

Everybody looks at Hormone to see where he's going with this, when Doc adds, "I think your diggin' in that trash for your dinner, aren't you, dirtbag?"

They all chuckle, and Hormone adds, "You're gettin' a little down-and-out takeout, aren'tcha'?!"

I look at them in shock. They're better at this then I thought they'd be. I try to say, "Yeah . . . look I gotta go," and walk past.

The Skeleton stops me and asks, "So what's for dinner?" as he grabs my backpack and rips it open. Pizza and meat loaf spill out onto the ground, and they all start laughing.

"Ahhh, nasty. You spilled his groceries!" EJ adds.

Nutt picks up a handful of meat loaf and disobeys C. B. by yelling, "Five-second rule, bitch!" and chucks it right in my face. It was fired at close range, and I wasn't expecting it at all, so it shocks the hell out of me when it smacks into my cheek and eye. Nutt's a pitcher on the baseball team, so the meat loaf had some heat on it. Tears fill my eyes.

All of my boys are cutting up when J-Low cackles, "Are you cryin'?"

I tell him to shut up and push him backward, before wiping my eyes. EJ shoves me into the Dumpster and my head smacks into the hard metal wall—*BANG*—"Don't touch him, dirtbag!"

I grab my head and feel a knot growing. A runaway tear flows down my cheek.

Doc looks disgusted when he says, "You're such a little bitch!"

J-Low adds, "Your pussy ass is always cryin', you know that?!"

That was uncalled for, so I yell, "No I'm not!" and try to run past. Somebody grabs my shirt, and it rips from the force.

"Where do you think you're goin'?" Bart asks, pushing me to the blacktop. "We're here to kick your ass, and we haven't even started yet."

They're crowding in on me, and C. B. moves his camera over Bag's shoulder. I jump up and grab the backpack before saying, "No, dude, I think we're good . . . You guys need to back up!"

Hormone pushes me and asks, "Or what?"

EJ demands, "What are you gonna do about it, dirtbag?"

I can't think of anything to say, and I think we've talked enough, so I swing my backpack and it hits College Carter Dumbass in the shoulder before splattering meat loaf all over the rest of them.

"AHHH!!!" They lunge at the same time and tackle me to the ground. "You MOTHER—!!!" They're hitting and kicking me all over my body . . . but they're pulling their punches. I tag College Carter Dumbass in the balls, because he left them wide open. I was so worked up that I may have done it harder than I needed to.

EJ yells, "Help the homeless, help the homeless!" as he pretends to kick me in the ribs. I'm flailing and grunting with the blows, but no one is actually connecting very hard (except me).

C. B. moves the camera closer to my face. College Carter Dumbass is rolling around in real pain, and Nutt grabs a handful of meat loaf and shoves it into my face as he yells, "Don't waste food, dirtbag!"

They laugh hysterically while I scream and try to get away. The meat loaf is rancid. "STOP IT! Get off me!" I demand, but they keep punching at me until I stop fighting and pretend to give up. I'm so out of gas!

EJ's gasping for air, too, when he says, "Dude—that was—pretty fun!"

My eyes are closed, and I think they're walking away until Brock exclaims, "Let's put this garbage back in the Dumpster," and they hoist me up and toss me back into the maggot pile. Dang it!

I hear them walk away, laughing and slapping each other five. I can feel the maggots squirming beneath me, but I can't move. I'm trying to catch my breath and figure out how badly I'm hurt. The camera comes back over the side as I struggle and slide my hands around the grime, trying to gain my footing. C. B. pulls his eye away from the viewfinder and says, "Awesome. Now lie back down so I can get a shot of you just lying there. Like you're knocked out."

"Dude?!" I say, and point to all the maggots.

He pleads, "Two seconds! I need this shot!"

I give him a dirty look and lie back down in the filth.

Five seconds later he yells, "CUT!!!" The crew, Abby, and everyone else explode with applause. C. B. yells, "That was awesome!" but I'm just lying there, wrecked, not acting. If I had an assistant, I'd yell at him to "Get in here and give me a hand!" but I seem to be on my own. Something squirms into my ear and I'm able to flick it out, but that's about all I can do. I may have fallen asleep or I may be hallucinating when I see Abby's head poke over the side of the Dumpster.

She asks, "Carter, are you okay?" and I give her a thumbs-up. She obviously doesn't believe the hand gesture, because a few seconds later she and Nick Brock hop into the filth with me and lift my worthless body out of there.

When I limp over to the craft service table I see that College Carter Dumbass has an ice pack on his crotch. I try to apologize, but he holds up his hand for a high five. "It was a pleasure; you're a great actor."

I slap his hand and try to joke with him. "If that was your idea of pleasure, you're pretty sick."

C. B. is still laughing in happy disbelief, and my boys are smiling with pride as they plow through the buffet. We slap and punch our congratulations as if we just won a big game. They're seeing how cool this acting thing is, and there may be a big debate in the fall: *Do I get yelled at in stinky football pads and possibly injured for life, or do I get applause simply for having fun and saying lines at the right times?* The drama department could be hopping!

C. B. takes off to set up his next shot. The guys are stoked to shoot their scene with Hilary, but I tell them it may be a while. I've tried not to go too crazy on the craft service table, but my boys aren't coming back tomorrow, so they make quick work of it. A lone plate of orange sushi is all that remains after ten minutes. I tell them it's pretty good and to try a piece. They wait until I swallow the slimy goodness before devouring the remaining pieces.

Phil walks up to give us an update, and surveys the damage. The empty candy wrappers, broken plates, apple cores, banana peels, overturned juice boxes, barren jars that used to contain nuts, cereal, vitamins, and dried fruit. He kicks an empty can of Coke and raises his eyebrows at the lady who's in charge of keeping the table stocked and organized. She looks like she's just been through a tornado.

Nick Brock burps, "S'up?" and Phil seems to realize that although my friends and I are pretty good actors, we shouldn't be allowed at the craft service table unsupervised.

He pushes a button on his hip and says into the headset, "Uh, we need a couple of P.A.'s to fly in for a craft service run . . . Now . . . Everything . . . Yeah, they ate all of it."

Matilda walks over and whispers into Phil's ear, but she's staring at EJ. Phil tells his assistant to take my boys over to the set right away. We're following him through the back parking lot, and Bag asks, "Why was that lady staring so hard at EJ?"

I reply, "Oh, she may think he's a drug dealer."

EJ stops walking and asks, "Why the hell would she think that, Carter?"

Phil's assistant subtly turns to listen when I say, "I don't know, you just seem shady to some people."

The art department guys have made the shop behind the auditorium look just like the trash-loading dock. Why the hell couldn't we have used this to shoot my scene?

Matilda and Hilary walk onto the set, and I give them a wave. The lights are all set up, so C. B. tells Abby she can take a break. He explains to the crew where the Dumpsters would be and where he's going to shoot. Hilary walks over and says hi to Nick before she grabs my hand. Matilda watches closely as my boys gawk with jealousy. I give them a wink and say, "Guys, you remember Hilary?"

They all introduce themselves again, and she's super nice. She's smiling, but she's fidgeting a lot and her hand is trembling, so I whisper in her ear, "Are you okay?"

She nods, and Matilda stalks closer to us. It's weird because most people see my boys and me as harmless teenagers, but this bodyguard obviously doesn't. To her, we are a dangerous threat. EJ is just staring at Hilary's chest, but Bag is trying to be charming and ask her questions. I guess Matilda's concerns are valid because guys in our basic age range are responsible for most of the mayhem in the world, and some people are legitimately terrified of that. I've started to notice people tense up when we walk into a room, and I wonder what it is that I'm giving off to make them feel threatened. I certainly don't mean to. Maybe I'm making it up, or I'm a little too in touch with my emotions right now. But when we walked into the Chipotle at the beginning of summer, I thought it was funny that the other patrons decided to eat on the patio. But now I think I may be bothered by it. Why do we try to seem so tough all the time? It's really exhausting.

C. B. interrupts my musings by telling the guys to come onto the set. Hilary lets go of my hand and follows them toward the bright lights.

Am I supposed to intimidate other people? Is that part of being a man? C. B. has all of those tattoos, and so do most of the crew guys. He wears dreadlocks, a beard, and has muscles like armor. What don't I know? What is so dangerous out there that I need to shield myself from? Am I supposed to be *more* Neanderthal or less? Lynn preaches respect and making a girl "feel special," but her boyfriend is textbook alpha male. My dad doesn't do CrossFit and isn't all tatted up, but I don't think anybody steals his lunch money. I guess part of being a man is choosing what kind you want to be. I'm not sure if you even have a choice, but at this point, I think I might.

I feel her staring at me before I turn and lock eyes with Abby. She's standing with Jeremy off to the side of the camera. She chuckles to herself because I was probably making a dumb face when I was lost in thought. She quickly looks away and tries to split when I walk toward them, but Jeremy puts his arm around her waist to restrain the move.

I give him five and he says, "Carter, I want you to know that your performance in that Dumpster scene was fierce!"

"Thanks, dude. I'm sorry that you lost your part."

He scoffs, "I'm already over it, and I've decided that I'm a theater actor anyway . . . or a costume designer. I'm preparing, as we speak, to make the outfits and star in the fall play."

"You figured all that out in the last hour?"

"Uh-huh."

Abby smiles again.

I give Jeremy a big ol' drama department hug and say, "Thanks for being you, J."

"Oh, you're totally welcome," he replies.

Being perceived as gay is one of my friends' biggest fears, but Jeremy is crazy gay, and although I like to make fun of him, I totally respect him. He didn't choose to be gay, and I'm sure it's a pain in the ass (no pun intended), but he doesn't apologize for it or try to hide from anyone. If I possessed half the confidence it must take to be openly gay in high school, man, my life would be a breeze.

He's explaining the plot of the fall play and how there are great parts in it for all of us. Abby nods in agreement, but I haven't even decided if I'm playing football next year. Hell, if you told me two months ago that I'd be at school on a Tuesday in late July, I'd have said you were crazy. Tack on the fact that my boys are here too, and we're all shooting a movie with Hilary Idaho, and I'd have called the D.A.R.E. officer on your crack-smokin' ass!

We watch Hilary and my boys walking out of the double doors for the third time. Matilda warns Bart, twice, not to touch Hilary, before she puts him in a headlock and he promises never to do it again.

Abby whispers, "So, is Hilary okay?"

"I don't know. Some days she's great, and others—"

"Have you smelled liquor on her breath?" she asks, really seriously.

I nod, and Jeremy gasps, "But she just got out of rehab!"

I reply, "Yeah, it doesn't seem to have worked."

Abby asks, "Is she doing anything else?"

I shrug and say, "Those pictures in *US Weekly* weren't what they looked like."

She laughs. "Yeah, we know, Starvados."

I try so hard not to smile, but it rips across my dumb face before I can get a hold of it. She is so quick! "I was just trying to say that I don't really know her that well . . . smart-ass."

Abby clears her throat and tries to hide her laughter.

She tells me that she's caught the aroma of booze on Hilary's breath twice. I decide to tell them about the overdose. I'm not trying to gossip; I really need to talk about it. I have to know if I'm doing the right thing by staying quiet, or if I'm being a prick by not sounding the alarm.

I try to explain. "Sometimes I think I'm being a bitch about it and it's not that big of a deal; you know, it's just something she does to help her feel a certain way. But other times—"

Jeremy has started crying, so I stop talking. He's not upset about Hilary as much as he is about a kid he knew that died from taking too many pills. He asks, "Why would someone like Hilary . . . someone who has it all—"

Abby doesn't offer up any advice, she just asks me, "What are you going to do?"

"I don't know . . . probably nothing. What can *I* really do? I mean, who the hell am I?"

She replies, "You're her friend. It seems like you may be her only one. If you and I have smelled her breath, then her bodyguard and C. B. and the producers have, and they aren't doing anything about it because they don't care." Tears well up in her eyes as she continues, "If you know your friend is doing something that will ruin her life, and you don't do anything to stop her, you have just as much responsibility as they do, don't you?"

Abby kind of breaks down, so I instinctively put my arm around her shoulder and give her a squeeze. This move has been off-limits for a while and I miss it. I ask her, "Are you okay?"

Jeremy jumps in to explain. "Carter, do you even know about Amber Lee?"

I shake my head as Abby leans some of her weight into me and sighs, "She and Rusty Dollingsworth are gonna have a baby."

My jaw drops. "Nooo. So that's why you're—that wasn't just a rumor on the last day of school, huh? That's some real deal, life-changing gossip."

Abby adds, "I knew she was hooking up with that greaseball. She told me that she wanted to get on the pill because *he* didn't like to use condoms, and she's so freaking insecure. But I didn't say anything, and now I'm trying to plan a baby shower that doesn't conflict with goddamn homecoming!"

I softly rub her back, and I may be enjoying it too much under the circumstances.

Jeremy tells me, "She was going to get an abortion, but her dad found out, so she and Rusty are getting hitched."

I sadly close my eyes and imagine Amber's Yosemite Sam–looking father ordering me to marry his daughter, and knowing that he'd kill me if I refused. I don't understand anything—how the hell could I raise a kid? I don't like Rusty Dollingsworth, but I feel sorry for his ass. I look over at my boys laughing with Hilary and goofing around. They're acting in a movie and having the time of their lives. They can't wait for the next party so they can brag to a drunk girl how they're celebrities now, and hope that the chick will be impressed/intoxicated enough to get busy with them—while Rusty is somewhere crying his eyes out, realizing that his future is screwed; that his part-time job at Jiffy Lube is about to go full-time; and hoping they'll make him an assistant manager soon so he can barely feed his fifteen-year-old wife and baby. Or the worst fate of all: he goes to work at Lee Auto Body, and Amber's dad is now his boss. He has to have lunch and joke around with the guy responsible for wrecking his life. Ultimately, it was Rusty and his sensitive wiener who ruined their potential, but I doubt the cops will see it that way when Rusty inevitably snaps and comes after his father-in-law with a blowtorch in a few years.

Abby seems shocked by how sad the news has made me. She lightly touches my back and says, "Really puts things into perspective, doesn't it?"

I finally open my eyes and say, "Yeah . . . she should've just given him blow jobs."

It was a joke, but she won't find it funny until she gains some "perspective" of her own. They say timing is everything in comedy, and what works for one audience is not guaranteed to work with another. My boys will love that joke, but Abby pushes me in disgust before she marches away muttering something. I look at Jeremy and shrug. "What?"

He holds up his thumb and pointer finger before saying, "You were this close, Carter."

21. SPIKE FAMILY

Toward the end of the day, I guess I fell asleep in my trailer, because my boys come in and wake me up. EJ says, "Yo, nap time is over. C. B. is throwing another rager. Let's go!"

Still in a nap fog, I yawn and mutter, "No, I can't ride that far, I'm too tired. I have to be back here at six a.m."

Hormone adds, "Suck it up, we're riding out there in the Escalades."

"What?" I ask. I can't believe Matilda would allow Hilary to go to a party.

Nutt barks, "Come on, pussy! We're in Hollywood now!"

I jump up and say, "Still in Merrian, dude," and walk out into the evening air, headed for Hilary's trailer.

EJ yells at me, "Are you kidding? You're not going with us?"

I keep walking and say, "I gotta take care of something."

EJ grabs my elbow and spins me around before he barks, "Yo man, we haven't seen you all summer and we show up here to bail you out . . . You're seriously going to ditch us again?"

"I'm sorry."

EJ shakes his head with frustration. "Whatever, dude. Do you know I broke up with Nicky two weeks ago?

And I haven't even been able to talk to my best friend about it."

That news causes Bag and Doc to high-five, and Hormone adds, "Thank God, the front seat of the CRX still stinks like Abercrombie and Ass." I have to fight off a smile. I apologize one more time and promise to call EJ as soon as I can.

I approach Matilda head-on. She's standing guard outside of Hilary's trailer. With disappointment I ask, "Are you really gonna allow her to go to a party?"

She seems deflated when she explains, "It's not my call anymore. I work for her parents and Phil Coates, and they don't want to me to restrict her anymore. The film wraps in four days; they've asked me to let her do whatever she wants and keep her happy."

"She doesn't need *happy*, she needs help."

Matilda shrugs as Hilary opens the door and bounds out onto the grass. "CARTER! Did you hear? I talked Phil into calling my manager." She gives Matilda a snarky smile and continues, "He informed my mom that my performance was suffering because of this police state/house arrest I'm dealing with. SOOO, we're going back to the lake house and we aren't drinking Gatorade this time!" She offers up a high five, but I leave her hanging.

Phil emerges from her RV and gives me a cold stare before walking off toward the production trailer. Matilda glares at him as he passes.

I try to ask, "Can we just hang out at my house? Or see a movie—"

But Hilary isn't listening. She's bouncing around and yammering away. "You're riding with me, okay? Ohhh, can we take your bike? Oh, I want to go off of that rope swing again and—"

I ask, "Aren't you tired?"

She shakes her head a bunch of times like a little kid, and says, "God no, we just had the best day; I'm totally flying! Are you ready to go?"

"No, I'm not. I can't."

Matilda looks at me for the first time with less than hate.

"Why?" Hilary demands.

I try to explain. "I'm just exhausted. And I really want to do a good job tomorrow and these last few days."

She shoots me a nasty look and asks, "What, and I don't?"

"No, that's not what I'm saying. I know that you're a professional, and I'm just a nobody . . . and I'm not trying to be cheesy or preachy, but I don't think you should go to this party."

She's not listening to me at all. She needs to go get drunk or high or whatever it is she needs to feel good about herself for however long the drug can trick her brain. You can see it on her face that she's going to keep pushing this agenda until she gets her way, and nothing I say is going to make a difference. She leans into my ear and passionately whispers, "If you're really tired, just go talk to Phil. He'll give you something, and you'll feel great and we can freaking go!"

She's trying to rush me, but time is kind of shifting into slow motion for me. I look over at my boys, standing next to the Ferrari, gawking. C. B. is entertaining them with a story and they're laughing. Lynn has jumped into Nick's truck and they're making out as the Skeleton and Bart chill in the back. Hilary snaps her fingers in my face and a lightbulb goes off in my mind. What the hell would Sport Coat Phil "give" me to make me "feel great"?

Hilary demands, "Go get your bike!"

"No—I told you how I feel, and I can't stop you from doing anything, but I won't be your wingman," I say as I back away.

She asks, "What the hell are you going to do?"

"I'm gonna stay here for a little while. . . . I'm still tryin' to work something out."

She scoffs, "Are you still trying to work on your character? We're almost finished!"

Hilary takes a deep breath to try to think of another way to sell me on her idea, but I cut her off. "You're a girl of quality. Do you know that?"

She seems confused by the statement, so I continue. "You're not a skank, you are not a product, you are not a brand, you are a girl—of quality."

The CRX starts up and my boys drive away. She watches them go and her eyes fill with tears as she mutters, "I need to go."

I throw up my hands and say, "I know. I'll see you tomorrow, I hope," and walk toward the production trailer.

She yells at Matilda, "Get your fat ass in the car! We're out!"

I knock on the production trailer door, and Phil's assistant ushers me into the office on wheels. I hear the Escalades rumble out of the driveway as we walk to the back of the RV. Phil is trying to look busy filling out stacks of paperwork. I ask him, "You got a sec?"

He says, "Uhhhh," like he doesn't, but then asks, "What's up?"

My heart is pounding, but I'm looking around the office like I've got all the time in the world. He tells me, "I'm a busy man, Carter. What do you want?"

I slyly ask, "Do you have any more of that ADD medication?"

He looks up from his papers in shock. His assistant backs out of the room, and Phil chuckles. "I can't believe you're not on it already."

I shrug. "My mom won't let me."

"Did Hilary tell you about this?" he asks, digging into his desk. "She's not supposed to do that." He looks at the bottle's label before he tosses it to me. I just stare at him and let the container hit my chest before it drops to the ground. His eyes slowly raise up to meet mine. Annoyed, he asks, "What are you doing?"

"Tryin' to figure out what kind of man I want to be."

He slyly smiles. He knows I'm here to have a serious conversation, but he tries to keep it light. "You think you want to be a producer?"

I ignore his question and say, "I think part of figuring out who you want to be is deciding who you *don't* wanna be."

He closes the drawer of his desk and clears his throat before saying, "Okay, so you got it all figured out? I'm the bad guy, that's what you think?" I shrug like I don't care. He adds, "You don't know shit, kid."

I nod because I'm aware of that one. He continues. "This is all fun and games to you, but it's a business. A competitive business that has very little to do with performances or character. I've got a time line and a budget, and I have to deliver a product . . . whether Hilary Idaho feels good or not. If one of my actors feels tired or anxious, it's my job to try to fix that. If they need to feel happy, sad, pleasure, or pain, and they can't get there on their own, I have to try to get them there. I don't do this for everyone, but I sure as hell don't need to justify myself to you. I think about little cute actor kids like you the same way a broker thinks about stocks. Some perform on their own and some need to be actively managed."

"That just sounds wrong, dude."

"I'm sorry, *dude*," he says condescendingly. "You think your friend Nick Brock isn't going to be asked to take steroids when he plays college ball? It's just performance enhancement, and it is everywhere. Everything is harder than you think, and everybody is looking for an edge. People who make things look effortless are just working harder and making greater sacrifices. C. B. works out like a UFC fighter, I drank ten shots of espresso today, and Hilary needs to go blow off some steam to keep her head in the game . . . because the first day we slip . . . is our last. We're professionals."

Tears are screwing up my vision, but I'm still looking at him when I say, "She's just a girl."

He doesn't respond to that because he obviously doesn't see her that way. Instead, he asks, "You know I've got three kids at home?"

I don't say anything, so he continues. "And I love them more than anything. I'd rather they made sneakers for a dollar a day then work on one of my movies or TV shows."

22. THE CRYING SCENE

When I roll up to my house, I'm so drained that I can barely pedal. But I hear the nail gun popping in the backyard, so I roll past the garage. It's dark out, but my dad's still busting his ass. He worked all day at his real job and came home to work on this stupid deck. He's lifting one of the last beams into place with his shoulder and holding a level in one hand and the nail gun in the other. The frame is just about finished. I hop off my bike and say, "Looks really good, Dad." I squat under the heavy-ass board so he can level and nail it.

He looks up and smiles before muttering, "Thanks, bud." The nail gun pops about five times before he sets the tools on the ground and says, "You look terrible; what's up?"

My head drops and I spill . . . all of it. He doesn't interrupt me, and he doesn't freak out; he just listens. When I finish he asks, "What do you want to do?"

I give him a blank look and reply, "What *should* I do?"

He shakes his head and says, "Wish I could tell you, but I don't know anything about this movie world. You're telling me about real grown-up problems here, and there's a lot of money involved. Kids aren't allowed to work for a reason. You signed a contract with these people. If you just walk out, I think we could be sued."

"So you think I should stick with it?"

He replies, "I'd never tell you that. I'd rather you and Lynn got jobs in a coal mine than go back to that movie set, but I can't—"

I feel bad because I can tell that my dad is upset. I don't know how much money I've made so far, but it's a lot. This money could help our family for years. We've encountered a new place in his parenting career, and he's not ready for it. We both thought he had a few more years of telling me what to do and knowing that whether I liked it or not, it was the right thing. Another problem he's facing is the million times he's given me his famous (not) "quitters never win" speech. Every time I wanted to bail on football practice or swimming or drop out of grade school, he'd talk me off the ledge and yammer on about the "unexpected lessons and gratification of finishing a task" and how my "decisions would affect people I'd never considered." We seem to have arrived early to the time in my life when I'm supposed to have heard all of his lectures enough times to know what to do . . . but I don't.

We walk into the house, and he clears his throat as he drops his work gloves onto the kitchen table. He's not going down without a fight (quitters never win). He tries to drop one more nugget of fatherly advice on me: "Basing your decisions on money or fear is always a bad idea. Some people let those two things run their lives, and there's a lot wrong with the world because of it."

I must be giving him a blank look, because he shakes his head with frustration and mutters, "I-I-I honestly don't know. Time usually illuminates the right path—"

I'm waiting for the "but" but it never comes. This is yet another reason they don't let kids into the adult world: My dad really isn't the expert I thought he was, and I don't think I'm supposed to realize this for a while. He simply advises me to try and get some rest and see what tomorrow brings.

I go to bed, but I don't sleep.

My alarm goes off at five thirty a.m. and somehow I stumble out of the house. We're back at Saur mansion for the pickup shots, and the crew is busily running around setting up for the day. The Ferrari is here, but no Escalade yet. I bypass the craft service table and head into the makeup trailer. My bruises have started to heal, or I'm getting tougher, because it barely hurts today. I head to my trailer and look over the day's scenes. There are a few walking shots and an easy scene where we talk about the writing contest. I wish we could have shot everything in order, but I guess it's impossible. It's a lot for my ADD to keep up with, and I'm as shocked as everyone else that I've made it this far. I've been so focused on this script that when I space off, I just drift onto another aspect of the story or my character. Sometimes I really think I'm going nuts, and now I know why Daniel Day-Lewis doesn't work very much.

The final scene on the list today is the one I've been worried about since the audition: the crying scene. Abby and I auditioned with this sucker, so I've known the lines for months. C. B. liked what I did that day, so much that he was able to talk the producers into giving a "nobody" like me this amazing part. But I have no idea how to get back to that place where I started sobbing in front of complete strangers. What happens if I can't get there? Could I be sued for not crying?

Hilary and I have rehearsed it with C. B. and McDougle

a bunch of times, but I keep forcing it. When I read it with Abby, I was so mad at her for flirting with College Carter Dumbass and making fun of me, that it bled over to the scene. I was angry but also hurt and shocked that someone I cared so much about could do that to me. I'm trying to think about Hilary and how screwed up her life is and how many people envy her and how cool she can be, but also how much of spoiled bitch she is. I think about how much she's let me down, and C. B. and Matilda, and the thoughts do make me sad and frustrated. But she's so guarded that I've never felt as close to her as I did that day with Abby, so to expect me to feel remotely the same intensity of emotion . . . I just don't think it's possible. C. B. keeps telling me to relax and just breathe. He thinks that my raw talent will kick in and I'll knock it out, but I kind of think that my raw talent = luck.

I'm trying to breathe deeply and shake out the insecurity when I hear shouting outside my trailer. I open the door as Sport Coat Phil is running across the yard. C. B. is right behind him. He's yelling at him like he's going to kick the crap out of him, but the two men jump into the Ferrari and tear out of the driveway, going about ninety miles an hour. They blow past the Merrian police car sitting out front. The cop just watches them go. (Man, I hope I'm a somebody someday.) The crew seems worried, but they continue to appear busy. I catch Abby staring at me, but she quickly looks away. I have no idea what's going on, but I know that I have no control over it, so I go back into my trailer and get back to my breathing.

I wake up about an hour later (I may have overdone the relaxation exercises) to the roar of the Ferrari pulling into its parking spot. C. B. is alone, and I wonder if Sport Coat Phil is lying in a ditch somewhere bleeding and wondering why he had to hire the toughest writer/director of all time. No luck; he's in the passenger seat of the Escalade as it pulls up in front of Hilary's trailer. Phil jumps out and barks orders to the gawking crew. Matilda slowly climbs out of the driver's seat. She looks pissed and embarrassed as she opens the back door, revealing a strung out Hilary Idaho. She's dead asleep, lying across the seat. I step out into the yard as Matilda grabs her armpits to drag her out. Mascara is smeared all over Hilary's face, and she looks like a drunken junkie hooker. Her eyes flicker open for a second, and they're glowing as red as her nose. She looks like she might puke, but takes a wild swing at Matilda instead. The big lady dodges the blow with the skill of a kung fu master and continues to move Hilary's skinny body forward. As her trailer door is closing, Hilary notices me watching the struggle. She looks away and then a scream echoes through the RV.

Eventually, the costume and makeup ladies go in, and yet another hour goes by. Everyone is staring at the trailer but trying not to. My sister and Abby are talking next to the craft service table, so I go over to get a Coke (not to see what they're talking about).

Lynn asks, "Do you know what's going on?"

I think about spilling my guts, but then decide not to.

Abby says to my sister, "Told you he was clueless."

Lynn shoots Abby a look like, "I'm the only one who gets to call him names, bi-atch!"

Abby looks slightly embarrassed when she says, "Well, I heard there was another party at Grey Goose Lake, and Hilary got really drunk and made a total ass of herself."

"Seems like you already know what's up."

Abby rolls her eyes, and my sister points at me as if to say, "Watch it."

I reluctantly ask Abby, "Did you hear if she hooked up with any of my boys? That's just what I need—for EJ to have sex with a celebrity."

She sighs, "You know, it's okay that you care about her. You don't have to say lewd things—"

I snottily reply, "Oh I don't? What a relief, I have your permission to care about someone. Maybe I could show my concern however the fu—"

Lynn throws a peanut M&M, and it hits me in the forehead. "Ouch!"

The trailer door finally opens, and none of us can believe our eyes when Hilary steps down in full prom makeup, hair, and dress. She looks like the cover of a magazine. She's awake and really, really alert. Her eyes dart around the set like she's trying to figure out where she is. Her gaze eventually lands on my shoes, and she stumbles toward me and my old muddy Nikes, as if we might know something. She's about a foot away from me when her eyelids close. I think she's fallen asleep, until they snap back open, and she leans on my shoulder for support.

Everyone is staring at her and waiting to see what I'm going to do. I brilliantly say, "Hey."

She looks up at me and seems shocked that I'm attached to the shoes she's gawking at. A lightbulb goes off in her addled brain, and she remembers that she actually came over here to bitch at me. "You're an asshole, you know that?"

My sister's head snaps to the side, but I put up my hand to call her off. I give Abby a nod and quietly reply, "Yeah . . .

I've heard that before. What makes *you* say it?"

She looks frantically into my eyes. Her face scrunches up, and I've never seen a pretty girl look so ugly when she yells, "You come on all sweet and introduce me to your goddamn family and friends and tell me I'm a quality girl—"

My sister and Abby judgmentally cross their arms at the same time, and I shoot them a "not now" look, as Hilary continues her rant. "Then you leave me all alone and you keep talking to my freaking stand-in all the time!"

She loses her balance and stumbles over her high-heeled shoes. I spring forward and catch her before she crashes. "Hey, hey, are you okay?" I ask as her eyes fill with tears. Her paint job starts to run, and black streaks wash down from her fake eyelashes. Her body is trembling in my arms like it's freezing, but her skin is burning up.

She looks up at me, smiles, and says, "Yeah, I just did a little bump . . . I'll even out in a second."

I look up into Matilda's eyes, and she can't hold my gaze. Her head drops and I notice that C. B. and the rest of the crew are watching us. My head shakes with disappointment as I whisper into Hilary's ear, "I don't think you should be here."

She pushes off me in a rage and snaps, "What the hell do you know about it? I'm here to work, not make friends or get your approval. If I don't work, my family starves!"

That seems a bit dramatic, but I don't say anything. She seems to be looking through me. She starts laughing and then crying again. "My mom is coming. Did you know that? Matilda called her because she's a sneaky bitch, but the joke is on her because she's gonna get fired over this."

I'm absolutely positive that Matilda is the only person

who really cares about Hilary, but I don't say that either, because she's stumbling around, yelling, "You think you're so cool, with your bicycle and your friends and your sister and . . ." She starts sobbing again, and it's hard to pick out what she's saying. Something about "pressure" and "one chance to prove . . ." something.

Phil's assistant eventually comes over and tells Abby that she's needed on the set. He notices the glob of mascara running down Hilary's cheek and radios Phil to fly over to the craft service area and figure out what's going on.

Hilary and my sister are staring at me like it's my turn to say something, so I try to explain. "I-I-I didn't really understand what you just said. . . ."

She sighs. "Of course you don't *understand*. You're a nobody! I thought you were my friend, though!"

Everyone is looking at me, wondering if I've got the sack to tell her off, or if I'll puss out. In past situations, I would just ask Hilary a question or two to disarm her and give myself a second to think up something good to say, but I can't think of any questions. I don't really want to know any more about this girl. I'm just trying to keep it real when I say, "Dude, seriously, you don't want to be friends with me. 'Cause if one of my boys was screwin' up like you are, I'd have to yell in his face that he's a selfish, stupid bitch! And I'd follow that with a hard punch to the shoulder. Your boney-ass arm would fall off if we were friends. You don't want to be friends; you just want another servant. You don't have a clue what friendship is about."

She isn't sure how to take the threat/lecture, so she just falls into my arms. I hug her quivering body as she cries. She's sobbing like a little kid and getting black stuff all over my shirt. Sport Coat Phil marches over to us and barks, "Come on, Carter, let's go!" like I'm causing all of this and intentionally screwing up his schedule. He's unaware that I'm completely supporting her body weight until he tugs on her arm and she flops to the ground. His eyes focus on the limp starlet's streaked face and my stained T-shirt. He yells at me again. "Damn it! What the hell did you do?"

I point to myself and angrily ask, "What did *I* do?!"

Phil ignores the question and picks her up. He throws her over his shoulder like a rag doll and yells, "MAKEUP!" like a soldier in a movie would yell "MEDIC!"

Ms. McDougle's car pulls into the driveway. C. B. and Abby walk over from the set to see what's going on.

Phil hollers, "Hilary will be out of makeup in fifteen minutes. If we are not shooting in twenty, heads are gonna roll!"

Matilda flies up and locks her kung-fu grip on Phil's arm. She orders him to "Put—her—down!"

He's not used to being given an order, so he doesn't follow it, but his elbow is being crushed, and he feebly whines, "Owwww! I need her! We have to get started!"

Matilda replies, "Stop! I will not allow you to treat this child like a piece of meat!"

Sport Coat Phil is as frantic as I've ever seen an adult. "We are so far behind!" he shouts as Matilda forcibly removes the limp noodle from his arms. He cries, "The investors are going to shut us down; we have to shoot at least twelve scenes today or we're through!"

C. B. has made eye contact with Ms. McDougle and drops his head in disappointment. We've never shot more than five scenes in one day, and that's a really good day. He covers his face with tattooed hands. He seems to have "lost focu" and thrown one too many parties. I thought he was so cool, but now I think I feel sorry for him. McDougle has been mad at me before, but the look she gave him was on a whole new level—vicious. I probably should have always felt some pity for him, though, because he missed out on a big chunk of his childhood and he's constantly trying to get it back. I know that a Ferrari is a cool ride and writing a book and winning the Cannes Film Festival is a big deal, but it doesn't turn back the clock. I'm sorry his awesome book will never be made into a film, but it didn't seem like Phil was going to allow it to be as great as it could have been.

I feel bad for Hilary because her life, as she knows it, is probably over. It may be the best thing for her, but she'll need a healthy dose of perspective before she'll see it that way. She's not even old enough to vote, but she was entrusted with millions of dollars and the reins of this movie. She's got everything and nothing. I feel bad for her family because they depend on her for their survival, and their meal ticket just punched out. I feel bad for the makeup ladies and crew guys and all of their assistants (not my sister—she's stoked and never wants to see an ironing board as long as she lives). I feel bad for Sport Coat Phil because he's the Artful Dodger and Fagin (bad guys who abuse kids in Dickens novels) all wrapped up into one super villain, and there's a special place in hell waiting for his ass. . . . But I'm selfishly crying for myself.

I cover my face with my untattooed hands, but I'm kind of blubbering, so I doubt I'm hiding anything. My sister gives me a hug, probably to shut me up, but it feels like she cares, and it only serves to make me cry harder. I start laughing for a second when I think back to how worried I've been about this day . . . the day I'd be required to cry. I start sobbing again when I think about what a dick I've been to my family and friends. I just yelled at Hilary for not understanding friendship, but I'm the a-hole whose best friend since kindergarten wanted to hang out yesterday, and I told him, "I'll call you as soon as I can." What a dick! EJ needed to talk to me about his breakup with Nicky; I should have dropped everything and begged him to tell me every gory detail . . . not because I have any advice or even remotely care. I should have listened just because he's my boy and he needed to get some pain off his chest. I start giggling again, thinking about how hard I've been trying to shed tears and how they're shooting out of my eyes like a fire hydrant now. Lynn keeps hugging me because I'm obviously a lunatic and I should not be released. I look up when I hear the door to the Escalade open and Matilda carefully loads Hilary into the back, possibly bound for the hospital, hotel, or airport. I have no idea. I'm sure I'll be able to read a version of what happened in next week's *US Weekly*, but I don't think I'll pick up a copy.

I think I'll be too busy apologizing to everyone for being such a dick and then doing stuff that *they* want to do (and not bitching about it). I'll have to mow with my dad, go shopping with Mom, do aerobics with my sister, play Halo with Doc, work on the CRX with Hormone, be Bag's skank wingman at the mall, watch pornography with Nutt (it seems like a solitary activity, but he's always loading up some donkey porn for us to watch, and even though I know it's bad for me psychologically, I will watch, because I am a good friend!). I will even listen to EJ whine about Bitchy

Nicky . . . doing exactly what we all knew she would do. I will nod my head and say things like "unbelievable!" even though it's not only "believable" but entirely "predictable." And a *polite friend* would never say, "I told you so." But EJ and I are *real* friends, so I'll say that phrase until I'm blue in the face. I'll call him a dumbass so many times that it'll still be echoing in his head in two years . . . about the time he'll try to forget what a hose-beast evil bitch Nicky is and attempt to hook up with her drunk ass at a field party. But he just might not go through with it because of me and the rest of his boys looking out for him. Because we matter. We may not be that important in the grand scheme of things, but we are positively "somebodies" to each other. I'm also going to take the longest, hottest shower of all time and sleep in a freakin' bed!

The Escalade rumbles out of the driveway, and I think Hilary may have sat up for a second and waved to me, but I didn't return it if she did. I'm so lucky Lynn is here. I'm so lucky my family is going to listen to me talk about these feelings until I don't want to talk about them anymore, and then they'll make me talk about them some more until they're satisfied that I'm good (or they can't figure out how to be any more annoying). I really do want to talk about this emptiness in my chest and the loss of direction I feel right now. I really thought that being an actor made so much sense, and now nothing does. I don't want to wake up every morning and go work at some job I hate. I don't want to live a boring life. And I thought I'd found this perfect loophole, but now that I've seen what it does to people and what the requirements are . . . I don't want anything to do with it. I'm not even sure I want to do theater anymore, if this is the endgame. I guess I could play football again, but that's depressing. If somebody is going to ask Nick Brock, the biggest, strongest dude I know, to get even bigger and stronger, what hope is there for a guy like me?

The crew watches as the Escalade turns out of the driveway. They seem concerned, but not like friends; more like their paycheck just made a left on Merrian Lane and is driving away.

An ambulance flew past the mansion a few minutes later, and that was that. My sister gave Abby a ride home, and I stole as much from the craft service table as my pockets would hold. I overheard Phil and C. B. talking through their options. I was chomping on macadamia nuts the whole time, but I'm pretty sure C. B. asked if he could reshoot the movie with me and Abby in the lead parts. Phil shot the idea down immediately and explained that *Down Gets Out* was now worth more to him as a tax write-off than as an art film. He told C. B. to try to write something else, because the only way this movie would see the light of day was if Hilary Idaho were found dead in the next few months. I don't think C. B. is as upset by this idea as he should be, but I know he poured his life into this sucker, and it's hard to let go. C. B. even asked what would happen if *he* were to die, but Phil didn't think he was famous enough for it to do any good.

Anybody need a used Ferrari?

FALL

23. CHEELLOOO!

I've been back in school for about a month, and I'm already failing two classes. The summer was a blur, and nothing went the way I expected it to, but what does? I sure as hell didn't think I'd star in a movie on the last day of freshman year. I made almost forty grand. The government and union took more than half, and what's left over will have to sit in a savings account for a few years. There should be more than enough money in it for me to go to college for a couple of years . . . before flunking out and moving back in with my folks.

One night, I'm supposed to be studying my geometry junk when the phone rings. I don't usually answer because it's rarely for me, but for some reason I pick up. Even though caller ID says that the number is "Unavailable CA," and I'm sure it's just some sales call, I push the button anyway and say, "Cheellooo?"

Whoever's on the line doesn't say anything, but they don't hang up, so I decide to flap my lips for a while (anything to avoid geometry homework). I tell 'em what I had for dinner and ask if they know what the hell a "hippopoto-noose" is. I hear a woman breathing or possibly laughing, so I add, "Is this one of those phone-sex hotlines . . . How does this work? I thought I was supposed to call *you*."

I definitely heard a laugh on that one, but then the line

went silent, like they pushed a mute button. The breathing starts again, and I only have twenty equations waiting for me, so I keep going. "Ohhh yeah, baby . . . what are you wearing? Oh yeah, you're just wearing a Snuggie, aren't you? With high heels? You're filthy!"

I hear the laughter again, and it sounds really familiar, like my sister's or Abby's, but not quite. Who the hell is this? A lightbulb finally goes off when Hilary says, "Carter, you are such a dork!"

I haven't seen Hilary since she left Merrian, unless you count that time on *Access Hollywood*. She was talking about her new album, *Hard Timez*. She wasn't as dolled up as she usually is on TV, and she held an acoustic guitar the whole time, but she never played it. My heart started pounding when the interviewer guy asked her about *Down Gets Out*, but she dodged the question the same way she ducked the inquiries about her parents and her love life.

"Hey, kid! What're you doin'?" I say.

She replies, "I'm just chillin' out in Palm Springs. Doing the rehab thing. Again."

"Cool . . . You sound good."

"Thanks, I am good. How are you and, um, Abby?"

"Good, yeah, I think, I thought . . . but who knows? You know how crazy girls can be."

She sighs. "Yeah."

"I know that we're not officially back together, but we did make out at a party last weekend, and now it's kind of weird. Neither of us likes parties 'cause there's nothing really to do if you're not getting drunk, so we just, you know, started making out, and I don't know if she was just bored or if she's into me again or what."

Hilary laughs. "She's into you, Carter. I'm sure you heard that Starvados and I broke up."

I gasp. "I did not!"

"It's true—it was all in the tabloids. But don't worry about me. I guess I'm hooking up with Tony Romo, who-ever that is."

"Good for you. He's a football player, and he seems really cool. But be careful—I've heard he's a player."

"Like you!" She laughs. She may be joking, but I like being compared to Romo.

"I am actually playing football again."

"I thought you hated it."

"Yeah, I did . . . I do, but I forgot at the wrong time and signed up. I just knew that I missed hanging out with my boys—"

The phone makes a crackling noise and numbers are being punched into the keypad really fast. I yell up to my sister's room, "I'M ON THE PHONE!"

Lynn's voice pops on the line. "Hello?"

I say, "Hang up."

"Who is this?" she asks.

"It's me," I say.

"Get off the phone, idiot. Who are you talking to? You better not be calling Abby after I specifically told you—"

Hilary interrupts, "It's not Abby."

Lynn demands, "Who is this?"

In a sultry voice she says, "It's Hilary Idaho. Carter and I were just having phone sex. Can you give us a minute, please?"

Lynn mumbles, "Oh my God," and hangs up quick, and I let out a high-pitched cackle that I've never heard before. Dang it.

Hilary says, "You were telling me about your friends and why you're playing football."

"Yeah, yeah, sorry about that . . . I guess I just missed hanging out after practice and talkin' trash and punching and getting punched. I missed the tackling and farting for the reactions and callin' someone an idiot and not seeing tears afterward. It made sense at the time, but I'm covered with bruises and I can't lift my left arm over my head anymore."

She's giggling, so I add, "I'm glad my life is so entertaining."

She says, "It really is. I miss talking to you. . . ."

There's a pause because I think I'm supposed to tell her that I miss her too, but I really don't, so I just stay quiet. Eventually she says, "Um, I was just calling to thank you for being my friend and trying to help me."

I nod as if to say, "Don't mention it," but she must not get it because she continues. "You were great, and I'm just working through my stuff here, and they want me to try to communicate with the people I care about."

I want to say something about that and try to capitalize on how much she "cares" about me. Maybe phone sex is on the menu after all. How do you have phone sex? Is the phone actually involved or do you just moan a lot and do your own thing—?

Hilary asks, "You know what I mean?"

I pry my thoughts out of the gutter, where they spend so much of their time, and say, "Uh-huh."

"My parents were just out here, and we talked a whole bunch and I feel really good, but part of this process requires me to reach out to the people that I may have hurt, and I think I hurt you, Carter."

We talk for a good long while about how I'm not mad at her and I'm glad that she came to Merrian and so stoked that I got to act in a movie (even if no one will ever see it). I try to relate to her. "You're not the only one who lost sight of what was important this summer, but I think we gained a pretty unique perspective."

Hilary agrees with me and tells me she's putting more emphasis on her music and has written a few songs that are really personal and "very Dickens." She likes the writing process and says, "It's really fun to reflect. You should try it. A sensitive guy like you would—"

"Easy . . ."

She giggles and says, "Sometimes things can seem insignificant when they're going down, but when you look back, you see how great it was."

I add, "Yeah, sometimes the opposite is true."

She's quiet again, and I'm worried that that may have sounded rude, so I tell her, "You can call me anytime . . . if you want."

"I'd like that. Thanks."

"Have you ever had phone sex?"

She laughs like I was joking.

ACKNOWLEDGMENTS

I must acknowledge:

My parents, Chuck and Charlotte Crawford, for their unending support and faith. They're painfully aware that they raised a complete dumbass, but they seem really proud. I guess the apple doesn't fall far from the tree.

My sister, Lindsey (Lynn), who suggested/ordered me to write for teen guys.

My editor, Christian Trimmer (if you've read my stuff, you should thank him too, because without him, it's pretty much unreadible).

My pimp/agent, Jenny Bent, and her former assistant Victoria Horn, who took me off the streets (unsolicited submission) and made me the semi-respectable high-class hooker/author I am today.

The Arts Incubator of Kansas City for letting me have a studio and leftover food.

All the girls I've loved before.

And finally, a special thanks to all the directors, casting directors, producers, studio executives, and their assistants for so rarely hiring me and allowing me to remain a starving actor long enough to realize my true calling: starving writer!

Thanks y'all! For realz!